Sarah Burlingame Rankin

Mariamne, Queen of the Jews, Genesis, Tree of life

The fairies, Centennial songs and other poems

Sarah Burlingame Rankin

Mariamne, Queen of the Jews, Genesis, Tree of life
The fairies, Centennial songs and other poems

ISBN/EAN: 9783337138042

Printed in Europe, USA, Canada, Australia, Japan

Cover: Foto ©Andreas Hilbeck / pixelio.de

More available books at **www.hansebooks.com**

Mariamne, Queen of the Jews

GENESIS, TREE OF LIFE (Edison),

THE FAIRIES, CENTENNIAL SONGS

AND OTHER POEMS

BY

Mrs. Sarah Burlingame Rankin, née Lapham

———·ᴑ✦ᴑ·———

CINCINNATI
Press of Robert Clarke & Co
1884

DEDICATION.

" Through the walls of hut and palace
  Shoots the instantaneous throe,
When the travail of the ages wrings
  Earth's systems to and fro ;
At the birth of each new Era, with a
  Recognizing start,
Nation wildly looks at nation, standing
  With mute lips apart,
And glad Truth's—yet mightier man—
  Child leaps beneath the Future's heart."

—*Present* **Crisis**, *Lowell.*

SKETCH.

The authoress is a native of Rhode Island, but by adoption a westerner.

Graduated from the Female College, Oxford, Ohio, when under the control of the Rev. John Walter Scott, D. D.

Married and lived thirteen wedded years in Covington, Kentucky. Then, urged by her only brother, Levi A. Lapham, a lawyer residing at Peoria, Illinois, she removed (1872) to that city. Here she engaged in arduous and unremitting study, laboring to deserve the esteem of the gifted and cultured people with whom she had cast her lot. With the same laudable ambition that moves the man of business to be identified as successful in his life career, the writer, whose only wealth is the acquisition of knowledge and the cultivation of an inherited gift, comes before the public in a pursuit which has ever proved the animating ally of education and good breeding, and the strong cordon of social refinement.

MARIAMNE, QUEEN OF THE JEWS.

For the account of Mariamne, wife of Herod the Great, consult Josephus' "Antiquities of the Jews," Book 5, c. 1-7.

Zedekiah was appointed King of Jerusalem by its Babylonish captor, Nebuchadnezzar ; later was carried to Babylon, where he died in prison. From this time foreigners made and deposed the governors of Judea, beginning with Zerubbabel, appointed by Cyrus. Under Roman authority, Antipater, an Idumean Jew was made procurator by Cæsar. His son, Herod, called "The Great," finally obtained the kingdom through the affection of Mark Antony.

This subject became our inspiration while reading the Antiquities. It was chosen and elaborated before knowing of its selection or before reading the dramatic poem on "Herod's Jealousy," by Calderon.

The reader must take the production with its stamp of originality which is the plainer synonym of afflatus or inspiration. To make the plot consistent, the poem commences with David, King of Israel.

THE moon full-orbed rose over Palestine
When David to the house-top moved his harp,
Boötes waned paler while the stars decline,
Arcturus glittering on his garter sharp,—
And few the marshals of the starry wards
Marching across the planetary court,
But when the bard makes melody with the chords
God gets the praises of the inspiring sport.

His Harp survives the Royal Jew !

                        The Land,
The Temple, Priesthood, Ceremonial, where?
The sacrificial-vessels, vestments, altars and

9

Their symbolic furniture evocate despair;
The Theocratic Polity has been fulfilled!
The Lion shall love the Lamb: The Child is at hand
To lead the Lion and offer the New Command:
The signs have changed, not God, who Omnipotent
      willed
To change His Will, whereupon His promises stand
From all Eternity.

                  Now Adonijah
Was feasting under the palms in Paradise,
The Royal Park crowned with th' Edenic tira,
A spot to allure and charm King David's eyes
When within its labyrinthal ways he walked,
. The conduct contémplating of Israel
Or enjoying Nature spiritualized and talked,
As Adam communed with this—and as him, fell.

"Nathan is here, O king, and brings thee news,
'Thy sons disloyal spread a feast to-day
At which Adonijah for thy kingdom sues,
Insults thy power and scepter, throne and sway,
Usurps thy Birthright, and begins to reign."'

This said Bathsheba to the king in haste.

"Solomon shall hew the traitorous crew in twain;
O prophet, there's no moment here to waste,
Upon my ass bear him to Gihon, where
Zadock the priest must anoint him in my stead
As king; the gathering multitude will meet him there,
Shouting, 'God save the King!' and making afraid

The rebels in yonder vale, and they will run
Suing for ' mercy,' from my lord and son,
Death will embrace the old king here in peace,
Jerusalem will flourish—Zion increase."

Thus David spake.

                 Moreover another king
An acclaiming populace to Zion will bring,
" Hozanna in the Highest to the son of David," who
Shall ride an ass and wail Jerusalem's Jew.

" Nation! thy glories all depart as spoil,
Drawing the lust of Conquerors to thee:
With anise, mint, and cumin thou may'st toil,
Serving the letter of the Law, to be
Hereafter cleft and broken, sawn and peeled:
My sheltering love, how often had it concealed
Thee from the doom impending, even as a hen
Appeals to her chickens under her wings! but, Oh,
Such love as mine thou would'st none of! again
Go, tread the wine-press all alone; for know,
Jerusalem shall be cloven from crypt to spire
And, piece by piece, be cast upon the fire."

*   *   *   *   *   *   *

It was night in David's city, and Herod kept
His vigil in the alleys of the Palms,
In that same garden to which rebels crept
To plot their deed of blood. The Leonine arms
Had been removed, for an Idumean Jew
Rules on the throne of Judah's Royal Line,

Roman emblazonries for preference sue,
Though Jewish sacrifices have their shrine.

A toga of purple wraps the Ruler's form,
A present from Cæsar, stitched with precious stones,
Around his forehead plays a jewel-storm,
Drawn by the moon, sailing high over massive cones
Of the Damascus date-palm, every gem
Glittering in his bandeau like imperious eyes
Flashing with fire,and plashing the surrounding hem
Of coppice with scintillations till there lies
On either hand a zodiac of light,
Through which he moves abstracted from the sight.

His sight looks inward—pondering his heart's maze;
Between his brows the forkèd frowns of thought
Darken his countenance, while a threat'ning plays
Like levin in his eyes; such threats had brought
If in the cloud the lightning sharp to flay
The queenly palm and Jealousy's fiercer ray
May burn as red across a darker day.

The swooping winds across the spicery snare
The aromatic smells of redolent wood,
Camphor, cinnamon, cassia are incense there,
And the tall aloe soaring into the flood
Of pearlaceous moonlight stimulates the air
Which scarcely soughs, so heavy with vesper scents,
The calamus growing by the pool, did spare
A spicy breath, with sweet sebaceous drents
Of nard, and Jiled's balsamic tree, balm sweet
Were all which filled this estival retreat.

Throughout the garden flowed a gentle stream
Knotting a crystal chord about the roots,
Giving at every loop a sparkling gleam
Among the brilliant flowers and verdant shoots,
A rivulet led from Siloah's fount,
" Going softly" through the Royal Paradise
Till o'er a reservoir's marble lip to mount
Purls down in cascade, sings its note and dies.

The king came hither, where the Summer moon
In all her glory seeming to be arrayed—
A Heavenly Sheba traveling at high noon—
Shone fully on his features, as afraid
He warily came, as shy of being seen,
Two doves were kissing, hidden in th' summery green.

An utterance dark—and then a heavy sigh
As if repenting what he then had said
Escaped his lips ;
              Night's stillness then did vie
With his stern pose,—when the weird coo had fled
Beyond his ear ;
              Listening ; he listened not
As the soft steps of woman's feet drew near,
His heart throbbed too wild, and his brain too hot
With anguish, that the light movement gave no fear,
And she came nearer, near enough to lay
Her hand upon the shoulder of the king.

" O king !"

He started, as a tigress may
Nursing her cubs, if a strange beast should stray
Across her lair :

Like blasting iron did ring—

" Woman ! "

It jarred her ear, that tone of ire
As it had bruised a harder thing than flesh ;
His eyes flashed like the sparks of steely fire,
His frame strained every muscle like a mesh
Which bound him rigidly, wavering and at bay,
In the presence of Salóme, sister of the king,
A feline whelp of Antipater—and only they
Who suffered her virulence felt how it could bring
The wounds, the torturing pangs, the deathly fears
Which strike to the life and poison as the sting
Of viper poisons; but her venom tears
And strikes the deepest, she who loved the king,
Mariamne, beloved of th' earth, for whom Heaven
      he sues,
Daughter of Hycanus, High Priest of the Jews.

That love is fatal which our fears can rouse
To jealousy, which every fear pursues ;
This snake in our love-garden, who can tell
Which is the fiercer, Love or Hate?   Two fires
Which are attracted, and combining, swell
The flames wherein the suicide expires.

The king drew life from Mariamne's love ;

Many children of his loins had filled his court
By many wives, though none to allure his love;
Herod proud, voluptuous, imperious, held his port
As a husband should before her, not a lord,
Love never led a man by a stronger chord,
As lion beside a lamb the two did go,
Twins born of a ewe, the nestlings from one tree,
Love fosters, grafts, but never prunes, we know
Love by excess but not by penury.

A wicked thought will escape and find its breath
Breeding infection or a blast of war!
Should the king die he had decreed her death,—
And Mariamne learned the secret, for,
Naught is so secret, but it in th' sun shall lie
And winds will carry it, and friends will cry
It from the house-top, and all the world will pry,
Even as the shock opens earth to let in sky.

Wrestling with constricting passions, on this eve
Herod turned to Kidron's vale while th' garden lay
Cooling in dew, and the full moon did weave
Every color and tint with her mild mordant ray
Fixing a lutescent medium softly veiled
About all heaven.   And the peach-almond tree
Felt its pink blossoms fade, Sharon roses paled,
Purple lilies put on black—the livery we see
That queenly star can most becoming wear
Royal yellow and black—these on the Labyrinth lay
When Herod came there, where his jewels flare
Like lamps among the alleys, every way

He seemed the corona for the eclipse of day.

The tormentress, who could turn the palace walls
Into whispering galleries of vindictive ire,
Hated the queen with all the hate that galls
At the sight of love like Herod's, as spirit to fire,
Torments the object of Mariamne's love ;
His feminine moods, his tender inanities
Entering the harem, taking no way to move
Save through the portal of Mariamne's heart,
Conjured up the demons of all the Insanities
In both.   T' sccern these wrong by wrong, each part
Unknowingly kissed the other to do a crime
For divided ends; the means secured a bride
For Heaven and him and all of Etern Time
Should prove and consummate the bridal; Pride
Conferred the power to make his beloved wife
The bride of sacrifice for this.   But to move
All Hell and Earth to destroy one hated life,
To pander a bride for Death, Salóme's power must be
Hate, Mortification, Envy, Jealousy,
Foes antagonizing heavenliness and Heaven.
The king's mad love men would have seen forgiven
As Time forgives ; for love is but the glow
Of God's Self-Attribute and undefined,
And men have crazed of love. this God to know ;
Have worshiped woman with as mad a mind.

Gentile and Jew receive the promises :
The one accepts the Messiah already come,
Another Interpreter of the Prophecies

The other believes,—and still for all there's room,

And God forgives.

                And now Salóme heard
For the first the king's decision ; from Sin's black spore
The Tartarean apple of love hung there and bore
Such prolification of jealousy, it stirred
Men's fears, knowing Herod's love tasted sweet before,
Until Mariamne's woe stained red with gore,—
As the Eastern Suri[1] snaps, like the wind's fair wracks,
Her helpness neck must stroke the murderous ax.

The problem of Existence here, when tried,
God remains God, though matter returns to dust;
The fool can read this truth; but, if denied,
Does spirit return to be from what it came?
Is there reunition of love with God as at first?
The Brahmin trusts his soul even higher, its flame
Refines in th' Nirvana[2] that absorbs its load,
Though this divine psychism seems lotus flowed,
Seems spirit inane as that on flowers bestowed;
Islamism prepictures the voluptuary's abode
Of Love unending: It is "love, love, love,"
Which souls have cried since Eons began to move.

But if the Christian's claim to Heaven must be
" Purification of soul," alone for his purity—
The Brahmin enjoys such a Heaven as this—just this!
To be wise, like God, would relate us to higher bliss;

He is truly wise, He surely is purely clean;
Have the works of God any stain to condemn, any
    mean?
Let Heaven be filled with these, then, O let man
Work out the problem of existence on God's plan.

The grandest works of men become their gods
Till hurled together in their common graves;
Things of men's hands and human like the abodes
Of foul corruptions which Destruction saves
Burying out of sight.   Behold how Herod died!
God compensates the worm with what He made;
The worm pulls down man's monuments of pride;
God remains God, and Spirit is Deified.
Strator surnamed Cæsarea, on the sea
Glistened like silver when the sun rose high,
Herod's marble city whose Roman luxury
The Imperial Mistress of the world could vie,
Whose noble mole outgrew the Tiber's pride,
Kissing the feet of Rome upon its shore,—
At whose full breast the merchant ships did ride
Gorging the voluptuous city at her door,
Whose Coliseum fills the marble stage
With gladiators, for the feast of Death,
Smiling as proudly on the assembly's rage
As though its umpire waved the victor's wreath;
And if the Jew wept over his Promised Land,
Sorrowing to see such impious pile arise,
Knowing his Law-Giver was guiltless of the command
" An altar for a human sacrifice,"
Purged his soul cleaner with his prayers and sighs.

God's mercy tempers even Jerusalem's doom!
When Jew and Gentile skulk along the street,
And the Centurions with their hundreds come
Bristling with glaves, and friends afraid to meet,
Or meeting eyes grow glassy, stiff with fear,
Face pinched and ghostly under the soldiery's leer,
Men petrifying as though the Gorgon sway
Of Fear fell upon all;
     'T is the doomster's day,
Mariamne's head falls by the lictor's blow,
Queen of the Jews and Herod's overthrow.

Hark! hark! what shrieks ring from Sebaste's walls?
What howls of madness, wailings of despair?
Jews use no racks; the rending wheel ne'er falls
Mangling its victim; what mean those shrieks there?
The fortress rings with Mariamne's name,
Court, gallery, dungeon, vault, and battlement ring;
Night roaring with the confusion, morning came
As horrible with din, and still more maddening,
With Herod calling Mariamne's name!
Behold him crazed on love, remorse, despair,
His love now fed by Hades' torturing flame,
Jealousy has fled and Crime confronts him there

" Her murderer":
    He calls, he roars, he raves!

" Call," gibber the seven demons of his brain,

" Mariamne's gone to Heaven, and there craves
No love from thee uxoricide, the Cain

Battens on thy conscience, ravening thee for love,
And Hell is just and thou must give him love."

NOTES.

[1] The rose of Syria, which was called Suristan, the Land of Roses.

[2] The first person of the Hindoo triad is Brahma, the creator of the world ; the second person, Vishnu, the preserver ; the third person is Siva, the destroyer.   But above Brahma there is the Nirvana into which the souls of men are absorbed after exalted transmigrations, and the attainment of neccesary purification for this absorption after death.

As the Nirvana takes precedence of Brahma, with this absorption the soul takes perfect repose and the enjoyment of all this Spirit enjoys in Eternal Bliss.

THE PRINCE IMPERIAL.

Nous recevons d'une de nos lectrices américaines les plus assidues, Mme S. B. Rankin, résidant à Peoria, Ill., une charmante poésie en anglais: *The Prince Imperial.* Cette poésie tout en prêtant un hommage au Français qui vient de descendre dans la tombe, est une véritable ode à la Liberté. Nous regrettons que notre connaissance imparfaite de la langue anglaise nous empêche d'en donner un traduction fidèle.—*Courrier de l' Illinois.*

WHEN Spring had warmed upon her breast
The violets, which the snows had pressed,
And curled the hyacinth's fragrant hair,
And sung the rose the robin's air,
An angel peered from out the skies
And thought our world a paradise.

A woman beautifully fair,
The gold of Castile in her hair—
Indeed, a very rose of Spain—
Was listening to the angel's strain,
When, awakening from the trance, she knew
The angel to her bosom flew.

She threw her white arms round its form,
She felt her wild heart, like a storm
Of passion beating the old love down
Since this new love was all her own,
Till her still eloquence, tear by tear,
Baptized the angel, "mortal," here.

Did heaven translate her in that hour?
This was the paradise of power;
The air shook with a joy intense,
" Vive l'Imperatrice et Vive le Prince!"
And banners blazed for them, as though
Heaven furnished its pavilion-bow.

The voice of fate was strong and clear,—
She lifted up her voice in prayer,
She walked no longer in a cloud,
The royal babe had made her proud,
For "a principality" she prayed,
And asked no lower of God's aid.

What was there that could be forgiven
In this white prayer, that went to heaven?
She only asked it for her son
The royal lily of her throne,
And every mother asks the most
That kin or country has to boast!

Millions on millions knew her prayer,
And prayed God " their first born to spare,"
Prayed Him, " that sweat, not blood, should flow
To give the grain its harvest glow,
Their red atonements make France free,
But not, a principality."

It was the common people's prayer
Rose from each fire-side altar there,
Bearing each Frenchman's soul to heaven,
Asking the least, that can be given

To help God's frail humanity,
But naught for principality.

Not for that cold but mighty head
Resting, at last, among the dead,
That would not let men be at rest
While he could hear the groaning breast
Of earth beneath his cannon wheels
Which lulled him with their thunder peals;

Not for that cold and impious hand
That slipped the chains upon the land,
Hurled his *coup d'etat* at consent
And mocked them with a President,
Nor let them see one stony tear
To calm their trembling hearts of fear,

Will sword and banner blaze again;
Although France has her iron men;—
For Freedom leases life too strong,
To yield kings this red-handed wrong,
And Time, dull, stony-eyed will see
A sphinx, of the Principality.
July, 1879.

GENESIS.

FAITH in God! a stern expression
Preached to believers in early time:
" Maranatha, or a full confession,"
Thundered the Canon Law for crime:
Pain has lost its fascination

For the man who kneels to pray,
Brand and scourge and mutilation
Amuse no idling bigots to-day,
Heretics robed *san-benito*
No court *Ex Cathedra* claims,
Auto-da-fé has lost its hero
Saved by this baptism of flames,
Rack and stake from mind we banish,
Iron collar, crown of snags,
Not a man dare think in Spanish
Of Religion using gags.

Once, the stars the Lord has scattered
Bountifully on the sky,
Some souls thought they there were spattered
For an ornamental dye;
The huge Opalescent Concave
Wore the polish of a stone
Which the fracturing fires engrave
With a thunder-spliting tone;
And the things they claimed as sponsors
For the young religious thought
Were 'the things that were the monsters
Recently from Chaos brought.

Then, the tree inlaced in corsets
Laced some maiden in its arms,
'Twas a lover's trick, to toss its
Purgatories at her charms,
And the lilies in the shallows,
And the echoes 'mong the hills,

And the torrents in their wallows,
And the wind's great organ mills,
And the waters of the fountain,
And the mists upon the river
Had their gods who made a mountain
Of our cosmographic sliver.

When man's only contemplation
Was a creed he could not read,
He refused the Revelation
Of the human mind to plead,
Thought his intellect a treason,
Thought the God of Wisdom bored
With the attribute of Reason,
Eve's lost attribute restored.—

Mind began its resurrection,
Broke away from priestly fraud,
From the sun's concentred section
This Copernican Sphere was thawed,
Through the diaphanic ether
Man could read the heavenly sphere,
Lyra's music sounded sweeter
When time brought the rhythm here,
Aldebaran's noble anger
At the Metador, concealed
But an intellectual slander
Of a scientific field,
And the nebula was something
Beside Berenice's hair
Which so long had had the trumpeting

Of a sacrificial air,
And the law of gravitation
Stars and atomies control
When, the spark of Inspiration
Touched the spark of Newton' soul.

Darkness fled when Fracastoro
At the baby-world did knock,
'Twas a Genesis he came to,
Fossils cradled in the rock,—
Since, we walk the earth's green door-yard
Graced with statues water-cut,
Read time's monographs upon hard
Granite bowlder, porphyry strut,
Propping up the sectile surface,
And the clambering stair of trap,
And basaltic column which trace
Of Time's lettering every scrap.

There's a Genesis of brotherhood
At the table of the Lord ;
Earth, indeed, has been the mother good
That has set us in accord
With the smoking tea from China,
Mocha ! O the Gods must dine her
Tutelary Saint of Yemem—
These have opened the world to freemen,
Savory spices from Malacca,
Ruby mulberries from the Caspian,
And the fig which seems to track her
Seeds across the tropic zone,

Grapes flushed with the fires Vesuvian,
Lemon-drops from bland Mentone,
And the date likewise commences
Where cooked victuals injure man
And can lay its proud pretenses
To Damascus and Iran.
We have spread our Constitution
For the table-cloth, our fare
Is the marvelous contribution
Which this generous earth can spare.

Minnesota shakes the pockets
Of her wheat-fields for their gold,
Earth can find no way to dock its
Bounty, which her coffers hold ;
From the bosom of Illinois
Rivers of milk and honey flow,
Round the world they do "Ahoy "
Her for all that she can grow,
She has fields of corn so ample
That her hungry sisters wait
Till her locomotives sample
It and bring it to the gate ;
California's banners flutter
While her northern cereals sweeten,
And her southern fruits do stutter
With their juices, when they're eaten ;
And the sugars of our tropic
Through as long a cane do flow
As would serve to make the tooth-pick
For a Patagonian beau ;

While the oranges of Florida
With the rice crop of Mobile
Grow upon the glassy corridor
Which covers up our keel.

O the morning star of Genesis
Points our residence in Eden,
It is gaurded by a Nemesis
'Gainst the disobedient heathen,
Where true learning spreads so ample
Every race within its reach,
Every man can pluck a sample,
We can print a book for each.

Praise to God! a grander Genesis
Has been heralded through earth ;
Christ proclaims his exegesis
" Love the price of heaven,"—Henceforth
Nations called to love and harmony,
Nations filled with joy and peace,
While His grand triumphant melody
Strikes the Heavenly key with these.

Time is something that's incipient,
God is never growing old—
Eternity is but the increment
Of to-day, which onward rolled
Its next Genesis to unfold.

PERSIA.

A POEM suggested by the presentation of the bust of Tom Moore to the city of Brooklyn by the St. Patrick's Society, May 28, 1879, on which occasion the union of Irish, Persian and American flags was introduced in honor of the poet of "Lalla Rookh."

HAIL, Persia, hail! thy royal name
Once the Koh-i-noor of nations,
Is richly blazoned in *sacred flame*
With Zend illuminations,
And sparkles like the evening's skies
With history's constellations,
Ere Europe opened thy grasping eyes
Thou asked Asia's oblations.

Men gave to Egypt a name to wear
" The mother, the eldest nation ; "
God selected an Eastern vale to bear
" The Paradise " of creation,
And somewhere planted mysterious trees
Where the tide of the green-gulf washes,[1]
Whose honeyed fragrance the blue-winged breeze
Round the realm of Eden flashes,
And placed man in the midst thereof
Ruling his heart with beauty,
The " Fallen Pair " in the legend of love,
For thy Gulzar[2] vales, might woo thee ;
For the women of Yzed[3] have a fame as fair
As their faces, which have no peer,

In wedded life, the charms they wear
Make man's only heaven here,
With **the** bread **that** he eats of Yzedecas
And the wine that Shiraz orders
And the violet lilies which stain the grass
'Long the gay Zayinderud's[4] borders.

The mightiest among men which **warr'd**
Thou hast begotten, O Persia!
Thy babe exposed, **to** victual a pard,[5]
Was wiser starred **than** Media,
For like the Eternal-Hand which strove
With the deluge at creation,
Cyrus humbled the world, as a sea, to move
For **him** of every nation;
His apotheosis left thy trust
Pasárgada's marble bier,
When Greece had halted round the dust
Which sleeps so potent here,
His shield, scimitar, and Scythian bow
Were all the tokens of honor
His tomb, when opened, had to **show**
The man who wept to conquer:
Hystaspes left thee to reveal
The strength of Persia's throne
His foot, visé found on his seal
Carved on Behistun's stone,[6]—
And are Persepolis' glories vain
Surviving common things,
Name, deeds immortally remain,
" Xerxes is king **of** kings."[7]

When the locusts of Mahomet
Swooped upon thee, like the horse
Of St. John, thou wast the forfeit[8]
For Death's, or for Allah's cause,
Over thy mountains, through thy valleys
Where the fire of Mythras burned,
How they poured, those lustful harpies
Filthier than the swine they spurned,—
And thy pure symbolic worship
Without taint or shame, was vext—
Just to please the harem's gossip
Or to swell the Koran's text ;
Nor can we to guilt confine thee
For indulging with the savage,
Christian nations look supinely
On his ravishing and ravage,
Cities, villages and hamlet
Know how Bashi-Bazouks murder,
Thanks, the northern tyrant lives yet,
Thanks to God for Alexander !

The poet has flourished his wand o'er thy vales,[9]
O'er thy flowers, o'er thy streams, o'er thy mountains
    and gales,
He has filled thee with music like sweet Israfil,
Who singing in heaven, the angel's keep still ;
He has found the blue campaka blossoming there,
Save, in Eden and thee, it's not found any-where ;
Like bright stars are the lakes 'mong thy hills and
    thy dells
Where the blue lotus swings to the wavelets its bells,

Or the nymphea blows open her vermilion-cup
And the gold-powered psyche sips all her love up,
Where the birds of the spice-wood build nests for
          their loves,
And the orchards are filled with the blue turtle-doves,
And the alma is full of its fruit and its flower,
Where it hangs all the year in the sky for a bower;
And the soil shines as yellow with lilies, as gold,
As each rain-drop a star from the heaven did hold,
And the serpent is charmed by the emerald's eye,
And the dew is too pure to transmit e'en a dye
To the scimiter, true to a hair on its edge,
And the fountains, like Zemzem's, complete every pledge;
Where the insects do sport such a regal attire
They deserve to be " damsels"—for each graceful gyre;
Where the maidens of Cashmere come out of the bath
With a skin like the tint that an Orman pearl hath,
Where the tips of their fingers are rosy as buds
Of the coral, the stain which the rich henna rubs,
With eyes looking mild as the sweet eyes of Alla,
With the dark shade that colors their soft drooping cilla,
With the spangles of campac which purple their hair
Like the luster of skies, when the planets are there;
But the rose of Cashmere can outrival them all,
" The light of the harem, the young Nourmahal."

          Persia, through thy veins the purple
          Of the Asian kings has flowed;
          Where thy common blood did gurgle
          There a love for freedom glowed;
          Gao's[10] veins were filled with iron

Like the Vulcan—of the gods—
Under whose ægis he turned the fire on
Which consumes all tyrants' rods.
Persia, thou art effete and weary
Like men when decay appears ;
Nations lose their pride as easy
When they live to die of years,
And, their battle-flags have feasted
The moth's epicurean taste,
And, their armaments are wasted,
And, their heroes' graves effaced.

Thou, voluptuous Orient dying,
Casting dust upon thy head,
With thy beard dyed scarlet, trying [11]
To deceive how near thou art dead ;
Isfahan, thy crown, how craven,
Hark, how reptiles nest in her !
And the birds of pray now raven [12]
On the sick Autocrator ;
Yet two spirits watch and ward thee,
Are the Prophet's cherubim—
Rose-dew sparkles on their poetry,
Are his dual seraphim—
Hafiz', Sa'di's wings upwaft thee [13]
Trimmed with love's enamoring fire,
Blowing the ashes from thy story
Christian-Freedom kindles it higher.

How sweet the songs of nations
Whose hearts are in accord ;

Their triune variations
Are one in praise to God;
Iran poured out a morning hymn
From her religious soul,
And when the sun's broad glowing rim
Toward the West did roll
Ireland's sweet harper laid his hand
Upon his golden-lyre,
Music the distance quickly spann'd—
The sun rose up no higher—
America caught up the strain
And sung the grand Antiphony,
The sun went round the world again
And Persia heard her victory.

NOTES.

[1] The Persian Gulf has been called the "green gulf" by Moore.

[2] Gul is the Persic for rose. Gulzar, a rose-bower.

[3] There is a proverb that, to live happy, a man must marry a wife of Yzed, eat the bread of Yzedeeas, and drink the wine of Shiraz. *Tavernier, Tom Moore's Note.*

[4] The Zayinderud—a beautiful feature in the view of Ispahan—is a river with no outfall. Tapped at every turn, and its waters led away to irrigate fields and gardens, the gay Zayinderud lies in the plains to the east of Ispahan.

[5] Astyages, King of Media, and grandfather of Cyrus, saw a vision—a vine appeared to spring from the womb of Mandane, his daughter, which overspread all Asia. When the child was born, the king delivered it to Harpagus, a person whose intimacy he used, who transferred the child to a herdsman to be exposed on the mountain.—*Book Clio, Herodotus.*

[6] The scarp of a rock in Persia, on which an inscription in cuneiform records the victories of Darius Hystaspes, who is represented as receiving the homage of captives, on one of whom he has planted his foot.—*Translated by Sir Henry Rawlinson.*

[7] On the platform of Persepolis is the magnificent propylæum of King Xerxes, with the inscription, "I am Xerxes the king, the great king, the king of kings."—*Translated by Sir Henry Rawlinson.*

[8] Revelation, ix, 7: "And the shapes of the locusts were like unto horses prepared unto battle."

[9] For "imagery," see notes to *Lalla Rookh.*

[10] Gao, a blacksmith, successfully crushed the tyrant Zohat, and his apron became the royal standard of Persia.

[11] In Persia old men dye the beard scarlet.

[12] The Shah's power exists by favor of England and Russia.

[13] The two great poets, Hafiz and Saadi, were both natives of Shiraz. The former has been dead 488 years, the latter 588 years. Their tombs are found in inclosures beside the path which slopes into Shiraz from the hills.

THE GYPSY QUEEN.

MATILDA STANLEY, the Gypsy Queen, died at Vicksburg, Miss., 1877, and was buried as Woodtown Cemetery, Dayton, Ohio, September 15, 1878.

In opening the poem we have used the idea in vogue when a youth, that the Gypsy came from Egypt, or was one of the lost tribes of Israel. It is now accepted that they wandered into Europe from India in the fifteenth century, and have since scattered over the countries of the West.

Up to the wild-wood with her
Gather the gypsy's quaint,
By our Christian rites, a sinner,
By nature's codex, a saint,
By society's creed, an outcast,
By their Egyptian blood, a lily
Pure as the one in Nilus glassed
Moses in his bulrush willy.

Into this green wood temple
Which rose without hammer or sound,
Under trees that dance and tremble
As Amphion's lyre was found—
Gather the mixed descendants
Of Copt or Indian blood
Or the tribes of Israel's tents
That vanished in Sechem's wood.

Nature in every feature,
Changeable as the wind,

Shy as the pretty creature
That favors the stag and hind,
Full of color and sunshine,
Cursed as the Judas-tree,
Free as the bear to dine
On the dish of the wilding bee,
Full of music as song-birds,
Up with the morning lark,
Melancholy as the words
Of the prowling owl at dark,
Homeful as the domestic robin
In the cherry month of June,
Harsh as the jays when cobbin'
Each other with quarrelsome tune.

Only the simplest fashion
From conventional man they copy,
The shady side of a wagon
Or an open and airy marquee,
A pot, a pan, and a griddle,
With a fire in the open air,
With a flue through the blue middle
Of the sky, the smoke to rear,
And like the winds, they pleasure
Around this zony world,
Packing along the treasure
They fugitively culled
From orchards and from vineyards,
From corn and melon patch,
And donkey after dark discards
The thistles for the cratch ;

As every wild-wood clan,
They naturally are free
To take from every man,
Nor stoop to beggary.

Children of nature, like their nurse,
With preternatural sight
They see the witches which disperse
A blessing or a blight,
They talk with river-ghosts which vail
Their forms in gauzy mist,
They know the Jack-'o-Lantern's trail,
The Echo's hidden tryst,
The cipher which the honey-bee
Has put upon his bank,
The witch-moss found upon the tree
With its polaric frank,
The wimple which the moon will wear
Before we have a rain,
The fish that leap, the frogs that swear
The gypsies' art remain,
The communistic flight of birds
Which follow round the seasons
Call forth their prophesying words
Without prosaic reasons.

Baskets of osier braided
And mats of woven rush
And fans whose feathers padded
The water-fowl with plush
They offer, with a hint about

" Your broken-bottom chairs,"
  Or ask to spell your fortune out
In the lettering your palm wears,
  Nor is their black-art spelling
Always so far from truth,
  But, we think that fortune-telling
Was the Endor's trade, forsooth.

When mansion, cot and wild-wood tent
  Had seen the ripened shock
Of corn, which, like pure gold, is sent,
  Put under key and lock,
Then Death, with th' sable shadows
  Following in his train,
Stalks where his potent arrows
  Hurtle, to find the slain,
On the Gypsy camp has fallen
  And taken a shining mark,
The clans have put a pall on,
  For the queen in death is stark.

———

MY JOURNAL.

Do n't you want to hear my journal,
  Where I write my life in keys?
I won't mind an interruption,
  You may stop me when you please ;

But perhaps you 'll find my story
  Like another's—I don't know ,

There is such a close resemblance
In our lives, of joy and woe.

Time has made the illustrations ;
Youth, restrained by flowery chains,
Tearing fretfully her fetters
When an iron chain remains.

Woman, reaching stars to crown her
Toils, to gain a dizzy seat,
When she suddenly remembers
Earth laid diamonds at her feet.

Then a pilgrim tired of waiting,
With one pale star on her head
Which at last must pay the obol
To the Ferryman of the dead.

'Tis a chain, however lightly
It is fashioned, if it warns,—
I have lived to love the roses
And to pardon all the thorns.

Turn this leaf of recollection
At the childhood of my heart :
Now the nettle's in the conscience
If I fail to act my part.

Pray, what is a faithful journal
But the open Judgment Book,
Where we truthfully should copy
Just the character we took ?

Here I babbled of a neighbor,
There I helped a scandal fly
For I listened without speaking
And pronouncing it "a lie!"

There, my heart was growing haughty,
Here, my look was growing proud
And I passed both men and women
As do people in a crowd,

And I wrote it here to warn me
Not to make myself a judge,
That to "look up and encourage,"
Had the world a right to grudge.

Not a blank leaf in my journal,
Not a blank day in my life,
Wrong or right, I've thought or acted
Up to human nature rife.

Love was breathed into a woman
With the spirit of her God,
Felt when she was led to Adam,
Named in honor of her lord,

She has proved its sweet fulfillment
Both in spirit and in law,
Adam till he saw a woman
Wondered " what was Eden for."

Over and over, love is the drama
Filled with mystery as then,

Just as tempting hangs the apple,
Just as sweet the sin has been.

Here I scorned a fallen sister,
God have pity on her soul,
How she struggled in her misery
'Gainst the tempter's wild control;

Men have preached and prayed and written
And sung " Poverty is clean ;"
I pronounce it here "a falsehood,"
Never blacker lie was seen ;

It has burned the cheek of beauty,
It has eaten out the heart,
It has poisoned every virtue,
It has deadened every part ;

I will preach it, I will pray it,
I will write it till I die,
That the curse of men and women
Is the " Curse of Poverty."

O this page is blurred and blotted
With my tears, tears, tears,
Love can fill the heart with heaven,
For its angels Death appears ;

I have had a cross laid on me,
On a tree I have been crossed,
And I wrote this in my passion
With the blood which I have lost.

Let me shut the book up softly,
Lay a mark here to be seen,
I have sat thus by the hour,
With my finger in between.

————

O, GREEN BE THE SONGS THAT INSPIRE THEE, OLD IRELAND.

O, green be the songs that inspire thee, old Ireland,
With love and devotion at home and afar,
A country denied to thy children's desire, band
They, maddening to rescue their emerald star.

Thy heart it has broken, while yielding to others,
Who proudly have wooed thee for mistress, not wife,
The sea and the ocean embrace thee like lovers,
O why the espousal, that's slavish for life!

Thy valleys and hillsides if blooming with harvest,
Or paling with famine, which stalks through thy fields,
Alike to the serf and the beggar the protest,
"The land for the lords, and the lords for the yields."

If thine be the sorrow, the shame by thy eggers,
To feast in the palace and starve in the cot
Has made thee 'mong nations a nation of beggars,
Thy masters have given thee this bastardized blot.

Not of sinew and blood has old Ireland been paupered;
The world has grown rich on thy bone and thy sweat,

In the armies of Ind where thy veterans are quartered,
Or laying the new world with Bessemer net.

And ever, wherever they fall to the windward
Of patriot, they answer the patriot's call,
And freedom is seldom seen drifting to wind hard,
But her foes have been shifted by Irishmen's ball.

When thy wit finds its pole, in the heat of the forum,
Its flash in the face of the Lion, is a shock :
As Burke with his eloquence held him a spell dumb,
Or Curran, or Grattan, or Phillips that spoke.

But why are their words like the pearls to the swine-herd?
O Ireland, thou fearest the strength of thy soul !
Thy bosom must release, at thy freedom, a free bird
To circle thy spiritual and temporal pole.

Thy soul must be free, as thy arm, to protect thee :
No fear of the judgment that follows the blow :
Thy God, be the Liberty come to defend thee,
Who suffers no vicar to ask for thy vow.

She comes an Immortal ! She comes from the burning
Which melted the fetters from church and from state ;
A cross had not held up the Christ, to the spurning
Of Roman and Jew, had she followed her fate !

She comes with the keys and the locks of the prisons,
The seals and the forgeries used at the dock,
While Conscience waves proudly her flag of revisions,
And Reason o'ertumbles the stake and the block.

She comes with the love of a man for his brother—
"And teaches the Earth and the Heaven are one,
The friends of this life are the friends of the other,
And Hell's broadest gate is what hate has undone."

With her for thy Virgin, and her for St. Patrick,
Thy heart shall be nerved, and thy arm shall be steeled,
And Ireland shall hail 'gainst the Lion, her bailiwick,
And beggars, and land-laws, and taxes repealed.

Whose harp can ring clearer, whose escutcheon shine
        brighter,
In the romances told of old England and Gaul?
Boast, boast! for one name could emblazon a miter,
Thy Wellington captured the Waterloo Ball.

Thy instinct, old Ireland, is hatred of kingship;
Thy sons find their glory where this finds a foe;
In war and in peace they inherit a sonship
With Mulligan, MacMahon, Montgomery, McDonough.

And ever, wherever they fall to the windward
Of patriot, they answer the patriot's call,
And freedom is seldom seen drifting to wind hard,
But her foes have been shifted by Irishmen's ball.

THE SNOW-BALL.

O! a fairy dance has the beautiful snow
    Tumbling from the clouds above,
With a flutter of tiny wings, so low,

We think of the arrows of love;
First *forward* and *back* and down *chassés*
    And waltzes, round in round;
It is a ball of the snowy fays,
    On their flight to the frozen ground.

Their gossamer dresses of snowy white
    Stream down the billowy air,
Each wearing slippers of ice for flight
    Beside the wings they wear,
Each crowned with a silver wreath of flowers
    Which bloomed in **Jack** Frost's hand
When he froze the mist into crystal bowers,
    Winter's crispy sunbows spanned.

Each starting for the Fairies Ball
    Goes light as a bubble of mirth,
Unheeding the realm where the wild winds call
    And whistle her down to earth;
The sprite who feels her slippered foot
    On the air's enchanted floor,
Must dance, as she felt her soul was mute
    To all but the dance that hour.

Still round and round in an airy ring
    With *forward* and *back* they go,
Till my terpsichorean muse must sing
    A dance for the beautiful snow,
Till bursting through the dismal clay
    Which fetters her wings below,
She flies, to dance with these frisky fay
    And turn to a flake of snow.

But what is the matter?   While she sings
   Her tune grows fainter and faint,
As though her soul had dropped its wings
   And ceased to be a saint,
Ah! there she lies on the frozen ground
   With all of the fallen snow,
Reminded each happiest soul is bound
   To its treacherous bubble below.

A'DIOS ESPAÑA.

AUGUST 3RD, 1492—AUGUST 3RD, 1884.

A'Dios España! cried a valiant crew,
   A'Dios, wives and maids!
Santa Isabel guards what heroes do,
   Every gallant Spaniard aids,
Viva! Viva! for the roving gales
   Which hurry our ships to sea,
Reaching the golden India vales
   They shall forfeit an argosy.

Viva! Viva! our Sailor Saint
   Is San Cristobal's captain too;
Men yield to courage as to restraint
   Roaming lands and oceans through,
Imploring Priest and King and Queen
   Confessing a rover's tale,
Jesus preserve him, bless him and lean
   Thine hand to his favoring gale.

Gracias! Gracias! for God's mighty space
  Of Ocean 'twixt shore and shore,
Nor ever Campeador did raise
  His courage higher before ;
If storms will threaten and calms will fright
  And compass too will fail,
The captain on sea will steer aright,
  The Lord with him remain.

*   *   *   *   *   *

Four hundred years ago, the sea
  Wore this western amulet,
Columbus found the divinity
  Then, jeweled from crown to feet,
And never adventurer on the sea
  Nor discoverer on the land
Has entered the lists of chivalry
  To accomplish a feat so grand.

The God of miracles made this west
  A Goshen of corn and wheat,
Ships follow the stars from west to east
  From the south and the north to meet
Columbia—where Spanish poet sings
  "Hope, is the fatal apple,"
Which sadly back to memory brings
  Old Spain's lost golden grapple.

SANTO COLUMBO.

WE would canonize Columbus,
   For our tutelary Pluck,
America would never do us
   Without Columbia, for luck.

Who his own canoe can paddle,
   Does believe that he did rock
In the very self-same cradle
   With the great Columbo stock.

Where you find the roof-tree planted
   And the family does thrive,
There you find the name is wanted
   For the hero of the hive.

Here, the school-house must be planted
   On this Education Rock,
And aside from this is granted
   To all dunces still a block.

If New Doctrine prove the obstacle,
   If the Catechism slip,
They have rigged the Tabernacle
   Just exactly like his ship.

By the compass of Faith to steer it,
   Sails of Charity unfurled,

And the rudder of Hope to veer it
   To an undiscovered world.

To rehearse our Country's story ;
   For Spain's splendor and renown,
She becomes the gem of glory
   Glittering in the Spanish crown.

I have traced our Spanish story
   In the Mississippi's wave,
Where the river takes a glory
   From De Soto's glassy grave.

Traced it, by a golden blossom
   Where in Florida it fell,
When it touched a poet's bosom
   It became Perennial.

Saw a Cortez like a comet
   Sweep the plains of Mexico,
With his Spanish sword did mow it
   With his Spanish fire did go.

Heard Balboa's soldiers trample
   First the Great Pacific Sea
And the Earth which grew so ample
   Was man's Star of Destiny.

Where the northern snow-storms bustle
   Down upon New England hills
And the western corn-fields rustle
   And the cotton softly fills,

There are masses by Historia
For the Cavaliers indited,
In each home the altar's gloria
Is "Columbo" when recited.

THE LIGHTNING EXPRESS.

BY A COUNTRY BOARDER.

LIKE a Cyclone astride its black racer at night,
On a catadrome dark as the River of Stix,
This Cyclopean horse, which is tamed with a light,
Thunders sixty straight heats to the hour—like a
    Nick's,
A tread like an earthquake, to make the ground shud-
    der,
A plume, which an old Demogorgon might wave,
Snorts of flame, like old Etna hurls up from his
    udder
Of fire when expelling his amorous slave.
With a rushing, a thundering, a bellowing afar,
Like a herd of wild buffalo scouring the plain,
Like a hundred drums beating the *reveillé* of war
You will hear at dead midnight the wild Lightning
    Train,
Like a comet blazed out on the black brow of night,
Like a meteor burst in the region of ether,
You turn blind in its stare of Gorgonean light,
Its Plutonean shrieks strike you mute as in Lethe.

While the cool lulling winds of the night are enchanting
The heats of the Summer away from your brain,
And Amor and Erato are tenderly planting
Dreams of love and Elysium, sweet solace for pain,
Lo! the bedlamite whistle has broken your rare ease
And fractured your ear—while the dreams of the Muses
Have fled, as the Lightning Train carried the Harpies—
Ugly, woman-faced birds, which belong to the deuces.

The Sun garnered up his hot harvest of sunshine,
The dew gently dripped from the black locks of night,
Quaffing draughts of sweet sleep, like somniferous wine,
I lay cooling, and dreaming, and wooing the sprite
Who was pouring her trifles of love in my ear,
When a shock to my sensories, pungent with pain
Dropped me down from the cloud, where the Muses
     appear—
I awoke, but to rave at the wild Lightning Train.
   June 26, 1884. Thermometer 96° in the shade.

THE ROSE OF PORTUGAL.

The poem is founded on a story of Portugal, illustrating the custom of not permitting sweethearts to meet until the paternal consent is obtained to the suit.

WHERE maidens blush through their tawny skins
   And lips have the glow of carnardines,
Where black eyes could be charged with sins
   If familiarly talking by dumb signs,

Languishing, flashing, smiling. leering
   Were accorded a confessional hearing,

A maiden was found to suit the tale :
   'Twas in the kingdom of Portugal,
Where genuine Port wine is for sale
   Which carries the name of the town to all,
Just where you would expect such eyes
   Were plenty after the Moor's rise

Or a beautiful Jewess could think
   Her's were the eyes we were singing about,
For Saint David left a link
   Which the Braganza counted out—
Hounded out—with their arts and sciences,
   Then raised nettles for church and penances.

The fact adheres, that Portuguese wills
   The first did shapen our argillous cake,
For a De Gama's ships were drills
   For the sea, like a true earthquake,
When he exploded Tormento Cape,
   And discovered the Earth's new shape.

You will find in a true love tale
   Just the pluck to conquer Ophir,
Portuguese captains did boldly sail
   To Brazil, then a Western loafer,
Charting unknown seas with new found lands,
   Helping the Lord with willing hands.

*   *   *   *   *   *

When we feel our passions tense,
   Sentiments morbid, emotions dumb,

Then we try the Persian sense
  To the love that is slow to come,
" Darling, dear, my angel, sweet "
  Feed the flame when sweethearts meet.

But in the kingdom of Portugal,
  Strange, with their warm southern fervor,
That love is mistrusted as too dull
  A passion for lovers to talk it over,
And love strategically is won
  Like a belligerent garrison.

A maid with a heart as rich and warm
  As a blood-red Rose of Portugal,
A soul as merry as a piper's shawm,
  Nor her's the exception, where in all
The fields and veñas the harvesters cheer
  Their labor by singing in roundelay clear.

But for a sweetheart she was dumb
  As the marble wife of Pygmalion,
A prevalent fashion of the kingdom
  Where lovers are kept apart, and one
Keeps watching the street from her window
  An admirer's pleading eyes to know.

And this in the land of Camoens;
  And beside the reigning king is a poet :
I have read a translation was his pen's
  Of Shakspere, truly he may owe it
To the bard who wrote so much of kings,
  A friendly interchange of rings.

But flirting with a hint, with a sign, with a token,
  With a rose dropped carelessly at the feet,
Sad soughings through lips that have never spoken,
  Palms clasping for hands which they never meet,
Brought the lovers to that desperate bid for com-
      passion
  Which ended this pantomime of passion.

The Church here, holds Saint Peter's place,
  Retains the key for a girl's admission
To heavenly love or its negative face
  Can equally send her to perdition,
Are its arrows dyed with her crimson pain
  'T is her expiation for every stain.

The wedding hour came round, and where
  We await the train and the marriage bells
And dancers to unweave the music's snare
  While the gay *bolero* faints and swells,
The troth was broken the ring united,
  As death was the only spirit it plighted.

But hearts were broken worse than all :—
  The rare old Moresque jewels' blaze
Was quenched in the sables on the wall,
  With the pride of the Olyssipolis' race ;
For the Rose had died of the love it bore—
  The Rose in the coffin, but not on the door.

*   *   *   *   *   *

Lord ! in thy name it is ever done
  Suiciding in Hell that Heaven be won,

As a lamb for the shambles love is slain
   With the body in bonds and the heart in twain,
With Cross and Nail and Thorn and Spear
   The Church keeps crucifying here.

Forced to a cell all bare and grated
   Went she, called "the Bride of Christ,"
With a human skull was mated
   God enveloped in bloody mist,—
Conscience dazed, and love a sob
   For the man the Church did rob.

Thirty years he sought the pavement,
   Took th' dumb lover's statued part,
Storm or sunshine daily there went,
   Carried an old man's broken heart,
While the nun grew old and waited
   Dumbly at her window grated.

NOTE.

In the Luclad we read that Ulysses, in his wanderings, is supposed to have reached Portugal, and that his descendents settled Oporto; therefore the people were called the Olyssipolis race.

THE OLD WIFE; OR, A MARITAL DILEMMA.

NEVER for you, the Old Wife's role,
Comb the curl from my silvering hairs,
Bind 'neath a frill, that my frigid poll
May mope the rest of my wifely years?

These memorials, now remain the best
Of th' orange sprays I wore, that hour
I modestly felt I could proudly rest
On your bosom, "a nuptial flower"
"Peerless" you said on our wedding day:
Do you prize it, as such, now my hair is gray?

It seems only a little ago;—
Time from every one will steal,
Even the blush, which a maiden will show,
Even the thought, which that blush will reveal;
With our consent, these, do seem to go,
When there is nothing, we try to conceal;—
Time steals the blush, the complexion, the hair,
Was it love, that you wedded, or only its snare?

Has the thrill died out of my heart,
Though the blush has died on my cheek?
Does no fire to my faded eye start?
Does the expression no praises speak?
You are troubl'd, that I'm growing old?

Dismiss the robber, that takes your bride ;—
For my beauty, a compensation you hold,
He is blinding you, while you talk of pride.

When the fire of youth is smoldering, then
We are falling to ashes, year after year ;
Till the dross has burned out of the gold, and been
Cast out to the carnal heap, we leave here ;
And we carry a heart without pretense,
A mind relieved of corroding care,
A spirit filled with a heavenly essence,
A countenance holier, for prayer.

In the heart of a song, love is ever sweet,
Our voices attuned this, long ago,
Our hearts did accord what the words repeat,
Our eyes did fill up the measure too ;
" Sweeter ; sweetest sing it over "
You requested like a lover ;
Now I'm old, to be my lover
Will you try to sing it over ?

By these shadows, I know I am growing old,
By this curl that is part of a youthful crown,
By the scent of death which the orange does hold,
By the song that is still, the tune that has flown ;
Yes I am old, but one day long passed
Never grows old, as the years grow old,
It was when my dead from my arms, at last
Went out with the coffin my heart did hold.

*   *   *   *   *

I know how love comes a wooing,
How his footsteps halt, pursuing,
How we catch the hesitating
Of his hand on the door waiting,
How we start, and go, and stand
And hush the throbbing 'neath our hand,
And check the tell-tale in our face
By putting on a stiffer grace.

I see favor presume to place
Love on a woman's manner or dress,
Beauty, which adds a softer grace,
Riches, which adorn unloveliness,
But my adoration's object
Wore the soul's imperial seal,—
This, the idol, of Love's project,
This, I worship, through woe and weal.

These memory bells, these memory bells
Sweeter with years and clearer with age,
Of the hallowéd past their melody tells,
The curtain of age is rung up, on the stage
The drama, is life, the actors are youth,
They come on and go out with their parts, in sooth
Nothing grows old, except women and men,
Nor too old, to go back to rehearsal again.

We can play it all over, the bitter and sweet,
We can freeze our tears in the fires of grief,
We can kiss the fetters which bind our feet,
We can carry a cross, if we seek relief,—
Yes I am old, I thank God for this,

I have given the rod a parting kiss,
I am walking a road which I never miss,
I shall pass into Heaven a child—in bliss.

Last night in dreaming of love
Angels were passing by,
With harps they floated above
On billows of melody,
They were singing of you,
I was dreaming from memory,
In my heart is the song and the angel too,
Must the Old Wife dream a threnody?

I am growing old and my years hold
Together like this ring of gold,
While I wear it there, my heart will glow
In renewing the vows of long ago,
Though I sometimes, ask of this ring, "if again
You would marry me over, if unwedded, as when
I was sealed unto you in the presence of men?"

———

NEWPORT, R. I.

WRITTEN in the Redwood Library, and copied, by request, into the
Register of the Institution.

Of all Earth's monarch's, here reigns one
Men never will disown,
God's seal is printed on the stone
Where Newport has her throne,

Her Royal Consort wears a ring
   Of costliest emerald
Jeweled so rarely, it will bring
   The wealth of half a world,
With this, he clasps her to his side
   Where love's wild currents flow,
The world will come to kiss the Bride,
   But leave her pure as snow.
December 6, 1883.

THE BENDING OF ULYSSES' BOW.
[Odyssey, Book 21.]

THE sudden transition of the narrative from danger and adventure to the spectacular scene, "The Bending of Ulysses' Bow," creates an ecstacy seldom enjoyed in reading a classic poem.

We trust the classic reader will appreciate our intention of giving a list of the suitors in the lines, preceding the verses in which Penelope having discovered her king and husband Ulysses in the beggard stranger, tries her strategem with her persecutors, by introducing the ordeal of Ulysses' Bow.

SEE proud Ithaca, the goddess
Of the consecrated isles,
Drunk on love and wholly godless
Maddened by a woman's wiles;
See the frenzy of the suitors
Gathering for the final strife,
Like Greeks when the clamorous rumors
Made the rape of Helen rife;
Look at impudent Antinous
The commandant of the train;

Eurymachus who would do worse
Seek with flatteries the vain;
Keep a watch on vile Ctesippus
Who did hurl an ox's heel
At the stranger, thought to truss
Him in Orcus like a veal; .
Set a spy on sly Melanthius,
That low goatherd of a thing
Who with slanderous tales and envious
Did insult his unknown king;
Watch the sneaking priest Leoides
Who the queenly bed desires,
It is Fate deceives his by-pleas,
Bland his lust—she knows its fires;
See Melantho's wild cotillion,
Threatening with a blazing brand
Him who dragged through fire proud Ilion,
Brought off Helen with his hand.

Then contrast the kind swine-tender
Old Eumaeus, who would spare
Every thing his hut could render
Worthy of the stranger's fare;
And the seer Theoclymenus
Saw the suitor's shades descending
Down where Orcus had a den worse,
Their compatriots attending;
Euryclea old and hoar
Whose young breasts did nurse her king,
Who detects the dreadful gore
On his knee by the mad boar,

Where the cicatrice does cling;
Loyal Philetius, the drover,
Kindling at the very mention
Of a chance to be the mover
For his lord freed from detention;
And the trusty, watchful Medon,
Who tells all about the ambush
Waiting for the prince Telèmachus
Whom the wily suitors will rush
To destruction with their black curse,
Ere, propitious gods Ulysses
Let return to pay avenges,
For his vengeance never misses
Any guilty hord's pretenses.

While, Penelope contends
With the clamors of the crew,
And her chastity defends
With a feminine wisdom too,
Day by day the suitors waited
On the warp her fingers drew,
Nightly was the web unbraided
And the garment never grew,
Till her maids disclose their torment
"That Laertes funeral job,
The jealous robe of ornament
Was contrived, their suit to rob;"
Baffled her wit, the queen must plan
To let the suitors know
The favoring gods have spared the man
Who bends the Elian bow,

Her challenge brings them all,—accursed
To touch the immortal wand,
The stranger's fate the gods have nursed,
He bears the immortal hand.

"It is the bow of **Ithaca**
    Which twenty loitering years
Has waited for a skillful hand,
    Shall conquer all your fears.

"Set up **the** silver circlets twelve
    A linear space apart,
The truest eye and steadiest hand
    Will pierce each circlet's heart.

"And those who press their ardent suit,
    Asking the queen ' to wife,'
Will welcome the impending fate
    Which hangs upon the strife.

"Unto the **suitor** who can send
    An arrow from the string,
And bend Ulysses' wond'rous bow
    And pass each silver ring,

"Shall be disposed these queenly charms,
    The queen's fidelity,
That all who hear of Ithaca
    Shall hear **what gods** decree."

The ordeal fixed, the princes spring
    To their appointed place,

Antinous, chief, then hands the bow
   Alternate, as they face.

The priest, the first, with saintly poise
   Must draw the silken string,
His hands have wasted all their strength
   The bow refused to spring.—

The next, accepts the stubborn **horn**
   Setting the singing reed,
Its strength resists his courtly arms
   Sealing his fate decreed.—

" Bring hither, slave, **the emollient oil**"
   Enraged Antinous cried,
" Rub, furbish **every pore** and part,
   Have gods **our suits** denied?"

'T is done—and still the Elian **bow**
   Resists their **heat of love**,—
Antinous yields his passion, which
   This ordalian test must prove.

The spumy lords smart, as they felt
   A burning rain of hisses,
The sting **is keen** when **they compare**
   Their weakness with Ulysses.
  *   *   *   *   *
" Permitted, I would try **my skill**,
   And doom the flying **shaft**
To pass the **medium** of the rings,
   My **fame once of this craft**."

They jeer to hear the stranger ask,
　"Perchance the fates command
That he should come to Ithaca
　To win the queenly hand?"

Penelope with ready wit
　Now soothes the indignant flame,
"He does the feat—a spear, a vest
　Rewards his unknown fame."

'Mid clamorous sneers, the slave then goes
　To hand the strifeful gauge,
And when the deft hands prove the arm,
　As fixed within a swage

It strains, it yields—the stubborn horn
　Seems the man's touch to know,
The shaft peals forth its singing note
　Ulysses bends the bow!

So helped the king of Ithaca
　His queen to keep her vow,
The missal draws the suitors' lives
　Ulysses bends the bow!

THE FAIRIES.

In a sweltering spell of August weather
When crickets fiddle their souls away,
When the mercury drops its silver feather
Caged like a bird, from its soaring way,

The flyers, the jumpers, as well as the creeple
Were watching a train of fiery cars,
When Oberon crept from his leafy steeple
Warning them, to run from the shooting stars,
When from hollows, hills, meadows, pools, rivers
    and swales,
From sedges, lushgrasses, ferns, flags and cat-tails,
Flew the stars of the Fairies, the fire-flies, and soon
All the Fairies were out in the light of the moon,
But the march was too short, for a song with a tune.

To rendezvous upon Clover Hill
Embroidered by a turquois rill,
An azurine lakelet, like a buckle
Upon its toe, laughed a mellowy chuckle
When flowery swans from fairy bowers,
Tossing about like a shower of flowers,
Bounding off, when they touch the brink
Of a wave too lightly, to feel it wink,—
Clasped each other—wing and wing,
And waltzed thereon in a fairy ring.

As I took the rustling wings to be
The fairies making a head-long race,
I made a screen of a huge oak tree
And taking within its arms a place
I soon forgot myself—to be
An elf in a tent of moonlight lace,
Which helped to deepen the mystery
And served to show each fairy's face.

With lances atilt to joust his neighbor
Each Ephemeron followed the rout away,
Like doughty knights flew every chafer
Making their wings like iron bray;
Behind—the Sphinx with stony stare
And lion-feet, on eagle wings
With dust as from a thousand years
Gathered thereon, in tawny rings,—
A cavalcade of mosquitoes come
Stunning all ears with their fify hum,
Their bills as keen as Toledo steel,
And prick like an awl in a cobbled heel;
The great stag-beetles brushed their horns
Against the branches of the grass,
In mail of shard the nettle's thorns
Felt soft as mosses, as they pass,
The bats flew round and round as tho'
The birds and beast should know each other,
The only fairy which I know
With an ornithorhynchus brother;
Behind these gravely marched two crabs
Xanthus and Arion from the sea,
Their trunks like a peddler's cased in drabs
Bore on their shoulders heavily,
These were two fairies from the sea
That promenade sometimes on land,
But not so fishy as to be
Compelled upon their tails to stand;
The goblins next—of all the fays
These are the ugliest and the funniest,
And just before the rainy days

You think their tempers are the sunniest,
The victims of inebriation
They drink of all the ponds and ditches,
And wear their tails upon probation
Then don a suit of leather breeches;
The lady-bugs in red and black
Had paired off with their beaux in gold,
And flew, instead of the mushroom hack
In which they rode when nights were cold,
When lady-cow fell in a flower
Which grew an inch below her feet
And floundering there for half an hour
Was almost fainting with the heat
Till lady-bird hopped on a fern,
Yelling so lustily for " help"
Her cousin lady-fly did turn
And laid the flower low with a skelp;
The gryllus strode like an awkward crane
Or jumped to keep up with the rest,
Of green silk coats, they are very vain,
With a swallow-tail, and a satin breast ;
But the brown grasshoppers were the wags
Who joked and teazed these prouder kin,
Ogling their fine clothes, until the lags
Were ready to die of a chagrin ;
Blue and green dragons—flies that look
Like Saint John's and Saint George's too—
Had steely needles which they shook
At Friar Boots, as past they flew,
A tilt of lances one might lose,
"Twas all the same—the fairy knight

Found that his lady-love would choose
His colors be they dark or bright
And these depend on day and night
And these were fairies black and white;
The glow-worm flaunted now a snack
Of livery differing from the rest,
Looking as fine upon her back
As though the blackest of the best,—
The love of color did appear
In fairies quite anomalous
Some brown and black and gray and sere,
Some painted like an omnibus;
And towering on their gawky shanks
The shepherd-spiders bore their humps,
Up-hill and down-hill playing pranks
Beside the worms upon their stumps;
Where all the spiders bridges grew
With a prison at each end of these,
A shower of little millers flew
Like parachutes among the trees;
Then, Mab drew near in gold and black,
A butterfly's ermine,—beyond a question
A match for Puck who rode a pack
He named "blue-bottle's indigestion,"
The last—but fairies are not dumb,
My ears were throbbing like a drum.

The bands blew loud and shrill and clear
Along this gay and weird procession,
I thought the whole created sphere
Delirious with the wild impression,

The trumpets blared until the moon
Though goddess of the elfin race
Turned suddenly pale as if 't were noon
And pulled a wimple o'er her face;
The trombones croaked until the sound
Resembled Egypt full of frogs,
The raucous croaking would astound
A younger fry of polliwogs;
The tamborines they buzzed and hummed
And kept up such a dreadful racket
All sounds were for some seconds dumbed,
The great dish-sky I thought 't would crack it;
The violins, treble, second, bass,
Together squeaked and squealed and squalled,
Things seemed to spin round—in a daze
I saw the tree upon me sprawled;—
While now and then a piccolo
Screamed out its notes so shrill and clear
The chitty elves thought 't was a blow
By some big Ouphe upon the ear;
Mine own buzzed like a pair of drums,
Whistles, fifes, fiddles, and jews-harps,
I thought the two great concert rooms
Would blaze with their electric sharps;
When lo, it was about the hour
Another king began his journey,
Oberon skulked somewhere to a bower,
The fays hid somewhere in a hurry,
With swans of silver, car of gold
Where clouds pink, primrose, pearl undouble,
Along the sapphire sky he rolled

Where all had vanished like a bubble,
And Clover Hill lay at my feet
The bees and bombus gathering honey,
I saw all elves were not a cheat
That these may think a man as funny.

———

LA FILLE DU REGIMENT.

PROUDLY marches on the nation
    Which its patriots will defend,   *
But remains a loyal station
    With its daughters to commend,
Cheerfully to send the heroes
    Who are called to field and tent,
Cheers! for those who hold the vetoes,
    Vive la Fille du Regiment.

How she springs to weave the banner
    With her fingers deft and nice,
That with freedom does inspire her
    And her soldier brave and wise,
Red and white and blue the union,
    Justice, Courage, Love are meant,
Cheers! for every loyal woman
    Vive la Fille du Regiment.

How she cheers the mustered heroes
    As they march away from camp,
As she scorned, to think of dire foes
    Who waylay them on the tramp,

While her vigilance perplexes
　　Even the soldier, she has sent,
Cheers! for her's the loyal sex is,
　　Vive la Fille du Regiment.

How she makes the weary marches
　　Where they rather die than yield,
How with tear-wet eyes she searches
　　For the dead upon the field
When, she reads the news which smother
　　Out the pride which victory sent,
Cheers! for every loyal mother
　　Vive la Fille du Regiment.

How the army's sanitarium
　　Prospers in her loving hands,
Homes, Sweet Homes, all recollect some
　　Far away in hostile lands,
Who are facing death and slaughter
　　For the help which woman sent,
Cheers! for sweetheart, wife, and daughter,
　　Vivent les Filles du Regiment.

How she bears the poignant anguish
　　In her tender breast, to go
Where she knows the dear ones languish
　　In the prison of the foe,
Ask not " who " or " who " have found them
　　After victory is sent,
All where heroines around them,
　　Vive la Fille du Regiment.

How her coming has translated
   Every soldier, when she staid
With the hospital and waited
   On the sick and offered aid,
Angels on their heavenly mission
   With no higher mission went,
Cheers! she has the saint's position,
   Vive **la Fille** du Regiment.

How she kissed their rigid features,
   Kissed the cold and stony hands,
How her sacrifice, will teach us
   What a country's life demands,
When **they bore** them and they laid them
   Where a **woman** can lament,
'T was a woman's love who saved them,
   Vive la Fille du Regiment.

How she hung the pall upon her,
   Looking sadder far **than he**
Whom **she** had brought home to slumber
   Under Earth's green canopy ;
It **is** woman, **tender** woman
   Widowed, orphaned, should lament,
War is to her the most inhuman,—
   Vive la Fille du Regiment.

When, Divine Justice hangs her garlands
   On the heroes of all lands
As Heaven musters up the thousands
   Of Earth's patriotic bands,

Heavenly stars entwined, like laurels
 For heroic suffering meant,
Will crown women with immortelles
 Vivent les Filles du Regiment.

DUST.

"IT is asserted by scientific writers that the Earth is a vast cemetery; that on its surface, which contains 1,853,174,000,000 square rods, have lived 26,627,843,273,975,256 inhabitants; making 1,283 persons to each square rod, or five persons to a square foot. A square rod is scarcely sufficient for ten graves, but each grave must contain 128 bodies.

"Thus it will be seen, that the entire surface of the globe has been dug over 128 times to bury the dead. How literally true becomes the declaration of the poet:

"'There 's not a dust that floats on air
 But once was living man.'"

I.

How mighty is the sphered dust
 Which is trodden under foot,
Made out of kingdoms, that the lust
 Of time destroyed their root ;
Made out of principalities
 Which took their stone and brass
And girded cities monstrous size,
 Which stood like withes of grass ;
Made out of monuments it seemed
 Would break the tooth of Time,
When Karnak o'er Serapis dreamed
 And the Sphinx was in her prime,
When men believed that strength and size
 Were the portraitures of God

And the Collossi leered their eyes
  On the pigmies of the sod.
Are **men** ignoble, that life warms
  Their forms of common clay ?
Behold earth gathering their forms
  Unto her breast to-day !
Listen, to the mighty host whose tread
  Is pressing green earth over,
Alas, 't is builded **of** the dead,
  Dust over dust they cover.
When Earth retook the lovely **vale**
  The site of Paradise,—
And men had made the green earth pale
  Where hanging-gardens rise,   .
Rearing Belus' confusing piles
  For priests and oracles,
Were millions turned into the soils
  Which built these miracles.
Where e'er on this broad earth we stand,
  On mountain, hill, or plain,
In green-wood wild, on desert sand,
  By river, rill, or main,
In presence of the eternal snows
  Or her perennial flowers,
The dust of tribes and races goes
  To make **this** earth of ours.
They are mightiest graves which Ruin fills,
  And mightiest tomb-stones story
The mightiest deeds, the warrior tills
  To gem his wreath of glory,
Yet, turned to dust, these look as yeared

As Old Creation's hills,
See Nimroud's cuneiform marbles spered
   Which Ashur's house rebuilds ;
For, when the touch of Ruin wrapp'd
   These in a royal gloom,
Palace on top of palace clapp'd
   A dungeon round their tomb,
Dust upon dust the mountain grew,
   City on city buried long,
That twenty centuries never knew
   It was Nineveh the strong.

II.

Count the nations which have flourished
   On the Asiatic main,
Count them by the Hindoo Veda,
   Of whose age no dates remain,
Century on top of century
   Piled these pyramids of dust,
Till the Earth—not Himalaya—
   Is the tomb, where they must rust ;
Count them by the heathen temples
   Sculptured in the solid rock
The Titanic past has builded,
   We are building block by block,—
Salsette, Poonah, Elephanta
   Have no dates to tell their age,
And the earth must keep the record
   Of their mortuary page.
It has buried living cities
   With its cities under ground,

In one night were lost the traces
   Where these places once were found,
When earth swept them with a besom
   That was fiercer than the sword,
When it vomited its fire
   And their swift destruction poured,
When the earth has yawned, and tumbled
   Twenty cities in its jaws,
Hurled the mountains from their bases,
   Burst them by volcanic laws,
When the mountains sent their torrents
   Like great rivers thundering down
And the villagers had fainted
   Like a blast upon them blown,
Blistering winds whose touch is poison,
   Famine with its lanken jaws,
Pestilence which breeds by millions—
   These at millions never pause,
Who are moldering on the hillsides,
   Who are crumbling on the plains,
And we walk upon their ashes
   Without thinking of their pains,
O, the traces of the races
   Who have lorded over earth !
Have become as smooth as places
   Which have never known a hearth.

III.

God breathed on a handful of dust. That breath
   Brought life to the common ground,
A single soul had earth that day,

By its heaven and conscience bound;
A single form, which in common clay
  Has planted a single grave,
A mighty usury, earth has asked
  For the little dust it gave.

WAR.

THE jaws of war are wet with blood,
  Yes, wet with human blood;
His whelps pronounce it " very good,"
  Lapping their tongues for food;
But did the God of Wisdom fail
  In making man a king?
That he, like every beast should quail,
  Hating this human thing?

Man only of man be afraid?
  Man by a man to die?
Then bolt the Book of God, that said
  " Man is like Divinity;"
Or lift Christ's bloody hands, and show
  The bleeding wounds he bore
Upon a brother's cross, and know
  The blood of Hate no more.

SCOTCH HEATHER.

By the wild North Sea, by the wild North Sea
  Once grew my Scottish Heather,
Where the hills of Aberdeen rise free
  And the firths flow close together,
Where Jedediah Clishbotham taught
  And kept the parish records,
And Effie Dean's sad fate was fraught,
  The Lily of St. Leonards.

The heather flower, the heather flower
  Is one of Scotland's glories,
To the Meg Merrilies, the moor
  Was like a bed of roses,
Or if, her wild feet brushed the dew
  Making the sun look late,
'Twas o'er the heathery crag she flew,
  Scenting Dirk Hatteraick's bait.

The heather-bell, the heather-bell
  Warred with the bold and valliant,
A flowery rampart, hid the fell
  Where fared the royal gallant,
When suddenly, the heather bore
  But Highland-bonnets blue,
"Saxon Fitz-James, usurp thy hour
  For I am Rhoderick Dhu!"

The heather-bell, the heather bell
  Thy muse is Caledonian,—
Thy minstrel loves her lyric shell
  Twined with thee, like a woman,
Though, verse that paints so fair a face
  From the features of creation,
Must e'er remain a modest trace
  And trait of imitation.

But Scotia gave another flower
  To twine with rose and shamrock,
A thistle-crown the monarch wore
  Where those wild seas are land lock;
Too, like the noble clans who fared
  Upon her thousand hills,
Thou wert—the emblem to be spared
  And feared, of, patriot Wills.

I could na tell how sweet thy bells
  That swing on braes of Doon,
Na feel love's heat the poet tells
  Let Burns to Mary roun,—
For all was love, that Scotia's bard
  Has ever sung or spurtled,
On Tam O'Shanter's mare he starred
  With Maggie cutty kirtled.

O heathery hills, O heathery hills
  Of Scotia's purple isle,
Thy jewels, every lake that fills
  The landscape, with its smile,

Thou art in Splendor, like the dream
That pictures Paradise,
Perpetual beauty, grand, supreme
In Faith that wooes the skies.

———

THE TREE OF LIFE.

TO THOMAS ALVA EDISON.

The world was chaos, where the Darkness throve,
Ruling the grand confusion like a god;
The lightning was his scepter, which then strove
With every part of the rebellious flood;
The thunder was his utterance, to make
The mass from center to circumference shake.

And Chaos had bounds, even as God has bounds,
Filling the whole of the eternal space;
And Darkness sent his sentinels the rounds,
Attraction, Force, Cohesion, which embrace
Like iron, driven through the surging flood,
Until the World was stronger than this god.

And darkness fled, and two great lights appear,
The one to rule the night, and one the day;
And darkness dropped into the sea of fear,
For even the night had grown a starry way;
And light was every-where, the light of sense,
And Light that spake, and is the God from hence.

And Light stretched forth his hand o'er firmament
   And the dry land grew green with trees and plants,
Prismatic with unctious flowers ointing with scent
   The atmosphere. A spontaneous life which wants
To flee the poisonous mists, which darkness spreads,
Inhales the light and its reflection sheds.

And light was beautiful, as it displayed
   All things which dressed the earth and walked upon it;
But Light was still more beautifully arrayed
   Than any thing, which from His hand adorned it;
And Light made man to be His holy image,
Asking His mind's subordinate for homage.

The Tree of Life still grows mysteriously nigh
   The Tree of Knowledge as they grew in Eden,
Man can produce and he can multiply,
   But if he could create, would this be forgiven?
The life, the germ of all created things
Indicates a mind from which all mystery springs.

If all miracle is done by Jehovah's sanction,
   (The visions of Bethel and of Patmos Isle,)
God's crystal ladders touch the heavenly mansion
   Which, glorified spirits passing up the while
Carry their crowns of sacred leaves, to show
His gifted ones have honored their gifts below.

Beneath this tree the bard of Khio walked
   Trimming his lyre with its spiritual leaves,
While 'round the strings his spirit fluttered, talked,
   Sung and caressed and the tree's mystery reaves,

Filling his isle with music, that was meet
To bring all Greece to listen, at his feet.

And from this tree, they took the garlands fair
   And decked the Roman streets and Capitol
When thousands shouted, "Bring the conqueror where
   Poets are crowned Immortal, when their crowns **are**
     full."
But Tasso, stretched upon his dying bed,
Visioned the tree in Paradise, instead.

This was a Gibbon's wreath, who climbed his way
   Up seven hills, to view the Roman world,
And from their dome, beheld her columns sway
   Till Pagan, Christian were to ruin hurled,
And all their dust rose up as black as night
And fell in seas of blood, before the Light.

These leaves, which grew from Spain to Eastern Ind
   And Western India, the discoverers knew,
De Gama and Columbus sought to find
   Where'er the Tree of Life, for healing, grew,
From Imperial Calicut to Mexico
The inspiring fragrance over seas did blow.

When, Genius tired of writing occult adornments
   And hieroglyphics in the burning East,
Worcester and Watt took up her costly ornaments
   To deck their motor which hard toil released,
And all the nations are with iron crowned
These God-like minds lifted **like** thread, and bound.

If the new Apocalypse is Bunyan's vision
  Newton and Priestly preach as divine a Word,—
"The light is rainbow, and the air's phlogiston
  Is living breath, vital as breath of God,
Earth is a prism for the Solar Star,
Her flowers the changing sunbeams of his car."

Struggling with laws of decay and development
  Man fills his heaven with what he can create;
The " Nature of the God " seems not content
  With any beginning and end,—like nature's fate,—
His labor and rest with time are striving still,
And man the factor of His creative will.

Thus man regains at last the higher life;
  Setting his face toward Paradise, once more;
When Franklin sent his key where clouds were rife
  With lightnings, to his creative mind it bore
A heavenly message of man's will o'er force;
Then laid the bridle in the hands of Morse.

And thou hast reached the mystery of voice—
  Which comes from God, and unto God returns,
Which leaves, a man as cold and free of noise
  As the dead rock, which mortal dust inurns,
Can sway and poise it like a tangible thing
Making it dance along upon a string.

Thou touchest, with fear, the terrene ear of man
  To listen if his God, afar, can hear;
Wishing his heart were better, than the plan
  He's daily following, lest his Lord appear;

Strengthening his faith, thou explorest the sensive way—
Songs of redemption to the dying stray.

Thy brow is glorious, which the Tree of Life
  Has crowned, which seeing, thou hast plucked and
    eaten;
Thy venture was toward God, who said—in grief—
  " To eat thereof is to live forever " in Eden;
This was but typical, shadowing from the sight
The Eternal Glory in the Eternal Light.

———

THE RIVER OF TEARS.

THE world is swept by a sorrowful flood
  The flood of the river of tears,
Poured from the exhaustless human heart
  For thousands and thousands of years,
It is sweeping thousands and thousands of lives
  On its currents, swift and strong,
O the river of tears, for thousands of years
  Has swept like a flood along.

O the river of tears, O the river of tears
  Is full of floating wrecks,
Some stranded on the shores of youth,
  Some, manhood tread their decks
Proud and ready to grapple with fate
  Whether sun or storm is strong,
O the pale wreck seen on the river of tears
  Shows the fight was fierce and long.

The river of tears, the river of tears
   Is lashed by tearful storms,
The isles of ocean would rend and sink
   If tried by the heart's hard qualms;
Blasting brilliant results like fire,
   Hurling down schemes like straw,
O the maelstrom of the river of tears
   Drowns the bravest, death e'er saw.

One haven has the river of tears
   With a Pharos always light,
All tears are wept ere we touch that shore
   No more to mar our sight,
A Father that's God or Lord or Christ
   Will clasp us by the hand,
And the flood of tears roll back in fear
   At the sight of the Happy Land.

CINCINNATI, THE QUEEN CITY.

Cincinnati's crown descends
   From her Aboriginal kings,
And her Roman pride contends
   For the splendor her name brings.
In a lodge of silvan birches
   Dwelt a daughter of the wood,
Her baptism paid the purchase
   Where Losantiville then stood.

Petticoated in a fawn skin
   Fringed with blue and scarlet feathers,
Stitched together with the quill pin
   Which the spiney hedgehog gathers,
And the crane bills strung like needles
   Dangling at her belt, to show them,
For the crane bewitched the evils
   And was the Miami's totem.[1]

Braided thongs her bare feet covered
   Of the badger's spotted coat,
Naught above her shoulders hovered,
   Save a necklace at her throat
Formed of humming birds which glisten
   Blue, and emerald, and gold,
And the sunbeams seem to misten
   Touched, her raven hair unpolled.

To Fort Washington they brought her,
   She became a soldier's bride,
Cincinnati is their daughter,
   Born to rule a queen beside;
And a great and flowery kingdom
   Trending westward with the sun,
Soon to yield a royal income
   With her was the dower he won.

And the red man could not save her
   When the white man laid the snare;
For the wiser ways are braver
   And the ways of God are there;

In the pauses of creation
  God still asks for "wider room,"
And the hand of civilization
  Makes the desert places bloom.

Lo! the wondrous change, enchanted
  Forests bow before the ax,
And the fields are plowed and planted
  As the springtime comes and tacks,
Till the summer's sunshine's drifting
  Down upon the Indian corn,
As the fruitful year is shifting
  Bringing round the harvest horn.

When the river like a driv'ler
  Only lay awake to dream,
And the bark canoe did quiver
  Like a lily on the stream,
The unlettered Indian never
  Its mysterious forces found,
Never could with reason sever
  Elements by laws profound.

But the virgin queen was smitten
  With an intellectual king,
When she saw his name was written
  On th' Ohio's wedding ring,
Though the pride and pleasure given
  For the present of the groom,
Sank as though the wrath of Heaven
  Buried Fitch beneath its gloom.

Lo! his altar fire is burning
  In his temple on the river;
Though no Stygian boatman's perning
  Now, the obolus of silver
Wafting souls to their Elysia,
  The prefigurement of bliss,—
The Ohio's Artemesia
  Made his mausoleum, this.

Lo! the ponderous steamer threading
  Like a swan the liquid floor,
And the vales and hillsides spreading
  Corn and wine and oil, and more,
Men are opening the treasure
  Kronos buried in the hill,
And are trembling with the pleasure
  Which did olden Titans thrill.

Queen of Industry! here planted
  And enthroned upon the hills,
Cincinnati's wealth is chanted
  By ten thousand voicing rills
When the clappers with their clamors
  Fill with music every steeple,
And the music of their hammers
  Praise the Lord and bless the people.

Queen of Art! divinely planted
  With thy sweet melodic shell,
Every air to be enchanted
  By a siren's witching spell;

Patroness of Arts! we name thee
    More than all the "Masterpiece,"
Flourishing shall grow the bay tree,
    Consecrated here, to these.

Since Ohio's noble mountains
    Were explored for their wealth,
And her river, from its fountains
    Has been traveled for its health,
And the years have left the harvest
    Heaped like gold upon its shores,
Men have kept thine honor fairest
    Which the page of history stores.
April 15, 1883.

[1] In searching for the totem of the Miamis, we found in Schoolcraft's Myths that "Twah Twah," the cry of the crane, was the Indian etymology of the word Miami. Mr. Newton, librarian at College Building, tells us that for an archery club who desired to take the name "Miami," and to use the totem as their insignia, he was unable, in his researches, to find the totem. Therefore we have assumed the crane as a poetic license until this or the correct totem is found.

THE MOUNTAINS.

WRITTEN in the cars while crossing the Alleghenies. January 11, 1884.

THESE mountains are a magnet, which appear
Attracting the sphere beneath them to the skies,
Mountains which cause Infinity to draw near,
Where stars draw closer with their glittering eyes;

Only the Eagle scales this dizzy height,
Embracing with the Sun, while both alight
Viewing the two Hemispheres of our World,
The Nadir's half, from which the light just rolled
Now sowing its ebon vault with relays of stars,
Like some vast Ethiop temple, toward which draws
The sable worshipers with flammeous torches,—
And the proud Eagle taking these mountain gorges
For the Earth's periphery, darts for a race
Making yon loftier peak their goal in space,
Too high to fear the cyclone's hundred hands
Pound bootlessly the base whereon this stands;
But Praise is winged for grander heights than moun-
    tains,
Singing "Glory to God" beyond the Sun's fire-fountains.

NIAGARA.

Written on first seeing Niagara Falls, October, 1876.

God sealed thee His, Niagara!
Omnipotence, His sign;
Clothed thee with His Potential Awe
Unutterable, divine,
And gave His Strength unto thy brow,
His Beauty to thy bow,
His Mystery to the ages thou
Hast rolled along, till now.

Thou wast ordained impervious
To Nature's softer sounds,
The voice, the song exalting us
Thy diapason drowns,
The electric tempest in the sky,
The bolts of death it deals,
Its thunder-volleys as they fly
Thy heavier bass o'erpeals.

Thou art High Priest of Nature here,
Her solemn rites attend,
And ephod-stones, thy shoulders rear,
Thy incenses ascend
Vailing with mystery thy throne,
Thy voice is raised to bless
Her worshipers, who hear thy tone
In deep devotiousness.

'T was the Eternal's hand reared thee
This mighty altar-place,
Of His most ancient masonry
Whereon Kronos we trace,
Thy Isles are water-walled and strong,
In the Almighty's plan
To keep thee priest of Nature long,
He made the form of man
To be a shadow on thy brink,
A bubble on thy wave,
A vision which a wink can sink
Into an awful grave.

And thou, like the Invisible,
Can'st span above thy head
A glorious bow divisible
Of the Sun's Iridian thread,
Lifting the clouds to the heaven which
Consecrated thee at birth,
When the firmament found its fountains rich
And poured them on the earth.

"Glory, glory, glory, glory,"
Seraphic in sun and storm,—
Thou art unlike the restless sea
Which loves its hours of calm,
But everlasting anthems raise
Like Old Creation's Saint,
Inspirer of man's feeble praise
Till our Star rechaosed faint.

VINEGAR HILL.

VINEGAR HILL, in Ireland, was the principal camp of the rebels during the rebellion of 1798. The prime mover and chief of the rebels in the county of Wexford was Father John, a priest who insulted religion by his cruelties and liberty by his crimes. Twenty priests celebrated mass at one time on different parts of Vinegar Hill, while the plundered cellars of the country around furnished the spirits for the occasion.

HAVE you heard of the place they call Vinegar Hill
    In the country of Ireland the county of Wexford?
You will both find it down on the map and you will
    Find it down in the book that's indited for record;

Like all the ferments of the Irish, you will
Charge them all to the spirits, on Vinegar Hill.

The Irish can swaten their tay with the tongue
   After kissing at **Killarney the swate** *Blarney Stone,*
And faix, do n't you know every man is half hung
   By the heels, **like Saint Peter, till the** *kissing is done ?*
For this pious shaking like a bottle, they still
Quaffed the more to the Saint, upon Vinegar Hill.

You can learn in few words that this Vinegar Hill
   Is famous for gaul, as the Gaul that bounds Biscáy,
Where the brave Father John camped his militants,
      till,
   He had gathered a crop of th' good Irish whiskáy,
Till the Protestants' barrels were piked and the rill
Had fermented the army on Vinegar Hill.

With pistol in holster and sword at his side
   And a cross of three feet to embrace in the saddle,
The doughty priest John did as valiantly ride
   As a Protestant trooper the devil could addle,
Be shure! All the saints he had mustered until
They came swarming to meet him on Vinegar Hill.

Instead of the Host, evil-spirits by the barrel
   Down the Gadarene troop how they slipped, in the
      storm,
They toasted men over the fire, in this quarrel,
   And the pike made the Protestants' cross of reform,
" For Jasus and Liberty " Father John still
Was imbibing the spirits on Vinegar Hill.

If Liberty wept upon Vinegar Hill
   For the smoke of the mass were her eyes never dry;
A covering of rags may be honorable, till
   They are thought the immaculate dress of the sky;
But the Friar with sword and with gun ever will
Be the Saint she abhors upon Vinegar Hill.

Justice even, sweat blood, as 't were her Incarnation,
   Her side it was gashed as the side of God's son,
But she balanced the cross in her greatest prostration
   And swerved not with pain, till her justice was known,
And the friars and the saints got as much in God's Bill
As she made out against them at Vinegar Hill.

.

THE DOOM OF FIRE.

" HOLY be the lay
Which mourning soothes the mourner on his way."

THIS poem was composed after the falling of the Ashtabula bridge, December, 1876, in which terrible accident, owing to the criminal carelessness of officials, three coaches, with all their passengers were burned, the loss of life being so complete that scarcely a vestige of clothing remained unconsumed. In this holocaust a cousin of the writer perished, a pocket pin-cushion being the only shred recovered and identified by his mother, of Des Moines, Iowa.

LO, THE vials of wrath are poured out on the land,
And the day of our doom seems already at hand,
We are shaken by terror, and broken by grief
And the earth seems to spurn every look of relief,
The tomb is refused, and the shaft is unreared,
Death-hardened, the vengeance of God is unfeared.

O our eyes have grown dryer than sand e'er the noon,
Or the lake wiped away by the fiery simoon ;
We are uttering the wail of Egyptian despair!
We are wailing the cry of poor Rama's wild share!
And our hearts 'fore the furnace of Moloch have sunk,
While the flames with the blood of our children, are
    drunk.

Are we stiffer in neck ? are we harder in heart ?
Are we charmed with our sins and our lusts ? till apart
With the followers of Dagon and Baal, we class
'Mong our Gods only iron, gold, silver, and brass ?
Have we shrunk to the size of the Heathenish King,
Must we walk through the fire, or worship—the thing?

There's a God!—though the ears of mankind have
    grown deaf
To the groans of the dying, the sighings of grief,
There's the mansion of God for the graveless above,
And the bosom of God for the angels we love,
There's the tender compassion of Jesus their friend,
And the kind ministrations which never can end.

Ye'll not turn to the coffin and bier with your grief,
Ye will turn to the Father and seek for relief;
O no, the cold earth has not given them rest,
But the flowers will again speak to ye from her breast
Of the beauty of heaven, the glory of hope,
Though the types will grow paler, wherever ye grope.

Ye will live in the spirit with seraphs and God ;
Ye will walk where the feet of the carnal ne'er trod ;

Ye will look far away from this clod and a stone;
Ye will learn how the visions of just men were known;
Ye will watch for the coming of judgment, nor fear;
Ye will go out prepared when the summons is here.

THE NEW ENGLAND DAISY.

[This flower is not found in the Western States.]

WHERE New England's vigorous clime
Fosters noble, classic rhyme,
Like a star that dropped from glory,
Stood the legend of Burns before me.

Where the clannish spirit stalks,
In old Scotia filled with lochs,
When the poet chanced to gaze
In the furrow, on its rays,
Seemed the plow his hand did gauge
To accept the minstrel's wage,
Like a harp his touch could thrill
With the afflatus of his will,
And the inspiration came
Like an ecstasy of flame.

And the plow seemed burning clear
Without either scar or sere,
As the bush on Horeb burned
When to flame the foliage turned,
And the daisy at his feet
Was translated to a seat

'Mong the Muses,—where it raises
For the poets, New England daisies.
FALL RIVER, MASS., *August* 7, 1883.

THE PLANETS.

INSCRIBED to Professor Hall, of the Naval Observatory, Washington, D. C.

Professor Hall, the discoverer of the moons of Mars, has christened his twin pets with the Homeric names of "Deimus" and "Phœbus." This fortunate American astronomer was lately voted a French medal, as the hero of the greatest achievement in astronomical research for the year 1877.

Two " singing stars" fondly appear
   Together in the evening sky,
Saturn sings tenderly and clear
   And Mars sings strong the harmony.

The very oldest songs they sing
   Of young creation and of war ;
The epochs only, time can bring,
   Who first the mighty singers saw.

"The Past," with recollection phased
   What the first noble voice can sing,—
When Earth stood blushing and amazed
   And numbered with his young offspring.

"Of Rhea" he begins to sing,
   When stern Succession wedded them ;—
" When Jupiter new-born did bring
   To Saturn his lost diadem."

And while he sings, a lovely throng
   Who now recall their father's voice,
Draw near, to hear the starry song
   And in his virile age rejoice.

Vesta who trembled in her youth
   To hear his winged feet draw near,
Has quite forgotten her mother's ruth
   Who hid the infant Jove from fear.

Ceres grows radiant, when she hears
   The golden-age again rehearsed,
The fire which warms the immortal years
   Within her golden seeds are nursed.

Neptune the grave, the silver-hair,
   Whose trident parts the threat'ning cloud
Among the clouds is seen to fare
   Where storms beat wild and winds roar loud.

And Juno her enchantment lends—
   Wrapped in the starry mist of night,
And to her father's bosom sends
   The arrows, of her eyes delight.

All are with song enraptured—but
   Another's thrilling strain, descends!
Like cymbals, clash the numbers shut,
   For hark! the martial theme impends.

"O'er Priam's strong mysterious wall
   Encircling his loved city round,

Mars' ruddy torch was hailed of all
  The Greeks in arms, upon the ground.

But ill-content to see the sway
  Of battle with the Grecian band,
He rallies Hector in the fray—
  And sinks by Diomede's hand.

Thus year by year he lit the tide
  Of conflict on the Trojan plain,
Till death to Hector did betide
  And Troy wailed o'er insulted slain.

When Persia leagued with death—her plan
  Arrayed her soldiery ten to one,
Mars was with every Grecian man
  Upon the field of Marathon.

E'en Christianity has named
  Him as defender of the faith ;
And the Mohammedan that's claimed
  By him, gains Paradise with death.

All nations ask his starry flag
  As ally round this spheréd world ;
Above embattled Malta's crag
  To death and glory 't was unfurled.

Those lands in winter armor bound
  Which scarcely feel the tread of war,
And those where flowers spring from the ground
  Enriched by blood his followers draw."

But as I list, the martial star
  Sings faint and fainter in the arch,
May be the olden spirit of war
  Is failing in the lovely torch,—

But hark! it strikes another theme,
  Trichoral music fills the air,
Orbs rise from heaven's celestial dream
  Flashing like cimeters were there.

And song on song breaks into spray
  Till sung by all the crystal spheres,
For Hall was born upon this day
  To immortality of years.
PEORIA, ILLS., *September* 3, 1877.

WHISTLING VERSUS KISSING.

THE TWENTY-SEVENTH LETTER.

A NOTE from Dr. Oliver Wendell Holmes on "the twenty-seventh letter of the alphabet" is published by the Indianapolis *News.* The correspondent who sends it to the *News* says: "I begged it for the *News.*" It is evident that Dr. Holmes was impressed with the character of the fair inquirer's letter, and answered it, believing Lavinia (which is the second name of Miss ——, a worthy member of the Society of Friends) to be a lady, but his P. S. seems to indicate that he half believed himself sold as to the sex. I will first give you a note of explanation sent us by Lavinia:

"The inclosed letter of Dr. Holmes was called forth by the following circumstance: 'Cousin Edward' and I were reading with much interest the story of 'Elsie Venner,' as it came out in the *Atlantic Monthly.* One day he asked me: 'What does Dr. Holmes mean by the twenty-seventh letter of the alphabet?' and when I answered he was not satisfied, and insisted I should write and ask the illustrious author for an explanation. To my inquiry the poet kindly sent me this witty reply. My willingness to gratify thy expressed wish prevails, and I place it at thy disposal. With great respect, 'LAVINIA.'"

BOSTON, *March* 4, 1861.

"MY DEAR MISS LAVINIA: The twenty-seventh letter of the alphabet is pronounced by applying the lips of the person speaking it to the cheek of a friend and puckering and parting the same with a peculiar explosive sound. 'Cousin Edward' will show you how to speak this labial consonant, no doubt, and allow you to show your proficiency by practicing it with your lips against his cheek. For further information you had better consult your gra'mma. Very truly yours, O. W. HOLMES.

"P. S.—Are you any relation to 'lovely young Lavinia' who 'once had friends,' mentioned by Thomson in his 'Seasons.'"

WHEN the first lord of creation
Was aware he owned a whistle,
'T was a prime alleviation
When his nerves began to bristle,
Proving a boon companion, that
His island was not lonely,
Sparing him from discoursing chat
Which would have bored him, only,
For dialects were, there, uncouth
And rhetoric difficle,
And so he puckered up his mouth
And blew upon his whistle;
Brutes pranced across the everglade,
Fish set their fins to quivering
Charmed by that first sweet windy trade
Which set the bugle shivering.
We read that Satan's speech began
In English or in Dutch,
But cursed as an ophidian
He had no use for such,

A trick of Old Theogony
Leveling man with brute,
Born with a like phrenology—
And springing from one root,—
But error often proves the fact,
This proves man has a Soul,
A Conscience, Dialect, and Tact,
Religion and Control.

But I am not for argument,
Offering this whiff of Reason
Where verse becomes its instrument
To ornament and season.

Ape tried his mouth-piece, though to grin,—
When Adam saw—this other
Was nearest like himself, as kin
In grinning, makes a brother;
So this young whistler spent his time
Twixt music and Orthoepy,
The only thing without a rhyme
In all this land of Poesy.
For the On-o-mat-o-po-et-ic claims
Of all of Eden's creatures,
He had a way to find their names,
By voices and by features;—
Which task accomplished, like a man
The woman-half at church,
Some entertaining work would plan
To give *Ennui* the lurch.

Musing of this, he dropped asleep,
When such a fog of glory
Over his jaded brain did creep
White, violet and rosy,
And such a head of misty gold
And flesh of alabaster
As coming freshly from the mold
In palpitating plaster,
Produced such joy, 't was like a wound—
Where his lone heart was bumping,
A fracture,—as, his ribs were sound
They seemed to burst with thumping,
Breaking the trance which bound his eyes
And ideal volition,
"Thou comest from from my side," he cries,
"I saw thee in my vision."
When Adam saw the pleased surprise
Her radiant face was succoring,
He felt his olden habit rise
He felt his lips were puckering,—
Eve was a woman, therefore wise,
Knew she would fail at whis'ling,
Gave to his habit, her sweet surmise
Puckering up her mouth for kissing.

GEORGE DENNISON PRENTICE.

THE SCHOLAR, THE POET, THE EDITOR.

THE writer is especially fond of Mr. Prentice's poems, **which are** strong, pure, and tender. And this was intensified by the writer's mother verifying a statement of his biographer, that Mr. Prentice taught a school in Smithfield, Rhode Island, which is her native place, and at her father's house he was a visitor, a brother attending his academy.

She remembers his fondness for poetry and some of the effusions to his early loves, which are not mentioned in his life sketch.

That Mr. Prentice will have lovers so long as books exists is undoubted.

The commencement of the poem refers to Prentice's oft repeated allusion to the "stars," which certainly are a type of the genius which steadily soared skyward.

The seventh stanza alludes to his lines on "An Infant's Grave," an emigrant's child buried in the forest of Arkansas, and which he met with and tenderly placed thereon a little flower to annually memorize his loving care. The poem is very touchingly told in the writer's own **words:**

> "'Tis well, 'tis well; but oh, such fate,
> Seems very, very desolate."

AMONG thy loved stars, I saw
  The brightest star of all, —
And earth awhile, the heaven, for
  Thy brilliant beams to fall,
Thou had'st more wisdom in thy brain,
  More beauty in thy eye,
More wit to lay thy mental train,
  Thy voice more melody.

Than hosts on hosts of other men;
  Thy heart the richest vein
Of friendship, always fuller for
  It flowed away like rain,
The sweetest sympathy, that made
  The music for thy deeds,
And gave thy poetry the shade
  Of pure religious creeds.

Crowned with the talents of thy mind
  The first of monarch's crowned,
Thy proudest conquests, were the kind
  Which in its toil are found;
And bearing westward, with thy star,
  The Nation saw thy hand
Flashing her signal-fires afar
  To her remotest land.

Wrapped in thy splendor, like a cloud
  Around thy person cast,
We then beheld the eager crowd
  O'er which thy spirit passed,
Th' earnestful, trustful, gladful throng
  Hungry for living bread,
Who felt their hearts and minds grow strong
  Upon thy wisdom fed.

But like the master of the ship
  When mutiny appears,
Thy thrilling orders sealed the lip
  On many a patriot's fears;

And steadied many a faltering rank,
  And strengthened many a heart,
And lived to see the fearful bank
  Of war-clouds all depart.

O'er thy magnetic glory beamed
  Thy soft, harmonious rays,
As Iris tenderly is gleamed
  Across the sun's strong gaze,
Bending as gently as she bends
  The poet's dream to hear,
Who, by thy fairer wings ascends
  Into a purer sphere.

Or weeping as a mother weeps
  Above her infant's grave,
Thy fount of tender feeling creeps
  Up to thy eyes, to save
The little stranger lying low
  Far, far upon the wild,
Planting a little flower to blow,
  As though it were thy child.

O, many a way gleams with thy "stars"
  Into the land of rest,
Where thou hast gone to make thy cause
  With the brightest and the best;
If thou hast been sublimed, thou know'st—
  Before the Eternal's seat,
Thy "stars" of genius are a host,
  Heaven's lilies round thy feet.

THE PHARAOHS.

METHINKS I hear the kings of Egypt laugh
While at Osiris' table now they quaff,
When—some full scholar wanders to the dead
Boasting of all the modern books he's read—
Telling "their stone primers, ages confused of Time,
To learn a letter or to read a line."

AT FRANKLIN'S GRAVE.

I WEEP upon his precious earth
But not one bitter tear;
Because he was of noblest worth
I sought his barrow here;
He was a master-piece of God
Made in divinest mold,
And consecrated is the sod
His mortal frame, can hold.

'Twas foreordained, that he was wise
In wisdom more than gold,
The thoughts which from his brain did rise
Were oracles of old,
He was the light of chaos, then,
The pillar and the cloud,
Freedom's apostle, helping men
To tear away her shroud.

What sacred sympathies were bound
Up with his giant mind;
Like dew of Herman dropping round
He cherished all mankind,
Casting into the common store
His glorious gifts from Heaven,
Enslaved Thought opened every door
And sent to him for leaven.

What wond'rous visions came to be
His pure Philosophy;
The mysteries of Earth, Sky, and Sea
And their cosmology;
Upon his ladder to the skies
Which brought the Lightning down,
What noble names thereafter rise
Upon his grand Renown.

Men serve their Destiny—and he
Began our golden age;—
His deeds did print immortally
Our own historic page;
Seizing the Pen, he led the van
Beside a Washington,
Giving the world the mightiest span
Of Architectural Freedom, won.

For him she spreads her starry wings
To chain the bolts of levin, .
For him her bow-men set their strings
Now, with the shafts of heaven,

For him the nation proudly strives
For letters and for men
To wipe toil's sweaty brow—by lives
Devoted to the pen.

MY OWN DEAR HEART.

My own dear heart, my own dear heart
　So light with love and joy,
What sweetheart makes me e'er so glad
　Or gives such sweet annoy?
Thy whispers are such tender, sweet
　Love-nothings, I'd not dare
To utter them allowed, they'd break
　Like bubbles in the air.

If once my lips begin, I pause,
　As every thought were still
Betraying the precious joy, I feel
　By some magic, of thy will:
I laugh with thee, I weep with thee,
　In all thy humor share,
No heart, except my own true heart
　Feels my love so little care.

My own dear heart, my own dear heart,
　Over thy thousand ills
Tear after tear more bitterly flows
　Than over another's spills,

Nursing thee, dear heart, night and day
　And giving thee relief,
I prove the truest, faithfulest friend
　Of all, who share thy grief.

My own dear heart, my own dear heart,
　Why should I prize thee less
Than other hearts, I prize and serve
　In happiness or distress?
Let me live true to thee, dear heart,
　Sparing thee from fault and stain,
I shall receive heaven's sweet reward
　And thou heaven's bliss attain.

My own dear heart, my own dear heart
　With its own small heaven is stored,
Love, from the holy of holies ta'en
　And scarred, like Heaven's Adored,—
Charity with all her attributes,
　Friendship which binds like brothers,
Esteem, which makes us love ourselves
　And desire the esteem of others.

MOUNT VERNON.

FROM notes taken during a trip through the States, including visit
to Exposition, we extract the following, written in Washington City
on the eve of a day passed in visiting Mount Vernon.

We stopped for some minutes on the lawn before the mansion, and
when we started to enter, felt like removing the shoes from our feet,
for it seemed to us a holy place.

The circumstance recalls our first view of the home of Abraham
Lincoln, at Springfield, Ill.; when, with eyes streaming with tears and
voice breaking with sobs, we dare not trust a reply to questions of
friends, who were kindly riding with us by the residence of the la-
mented president.

MOUNT VERNON! in thy sacred shade
   I wandered to and fro,
And over all the pleasant glade
   The past did come and go.

The knotted oaks in gray decay,
   The vines supporting these,
The asters blue along the way
   Were full of memories.

The high commanding walk which led
   Directly to the door,
The hill-side wild with nature, wed
   To all Potomac's lore.

The river rolling grandly on
   Down to the mighty sea,
Its waves no grayer, that have gone
   Thus many a century;

Yet every one that kissed the shore
    To history did belong,
The Indian sang his pow-wow o'er,
    The Englishman his song.

I lingered here and there about
    Pained still to cross the door,
Where th' disembodied had gone out
    Returning there, no more.

What was I! that I dare approach
    This shrine of love and trust?
The very mightiest would encroach
    Seemingly, on the dust;

And yet I sat me down upon
    The chairs, as though I knew
The occupant, with Washington
    To hold an interview;

I drew up to the table there
    As though I was a guest,
And viewed the pictures, with an air
    Of free familiar zest.

The doors stood ope from room to room,
    The crowd swayed in and out,
But it was struggling with the gloom
    To make the picture out.

For who were these? they were not Knox,
    Nor Green, nor Lafayette,

There was no woman, on whose locks
   The mistress' halo set;

There was no loftier one than all,
   Whose strong commanding glance
Reproved the virtues lax, or call
   Them from their painful trance;

There was no sweet commanding voice,
   Could start the noble thrill
Of pride in it, till the annoys
   Of vanity were still.

It fairly seemed as though the place
   Was held thus by a trance,
That surely, those great ones would grace
   Again the lordly manse;

I thought to hear the silver tone
   Of music through the house,
The harpsichord, but wanted one
   Light touch, of the fair spouse;

I thought to hear the servants' feet
   Both up and down the stair,
As Randolph, Jefferson, were greet
   As guests, and honored there.

The past was all embodied here,
   As of to-day a part,
And standing at the Chieftain's bier
   The grateful thought did start,

That pilgrim nations would come here,
   Vernon still unforgot,—
Though reconquering nature reappear
   O'er all this sacred spot.

October 16, 1876.

———

THE CHARLES RIVER BRIDGE, BOSTON.

EVENING on the Charles River Bridge, Boston, after a visit to Mount Auburn and the graves of Longfellow, Everett, Agassiz, Charlotte Cushman, and other noted American characters.

DAY stepped quietly into heaven,
   Furled her feathery beams of light,
As the Darkness climbed the mountain
   Listening to the owl of night.

From a silvery crown of moonlight,
   Heavenly spirits there might bear
High above the graves of Auburn,
   A mild radiance filled the air.

Under the milky-way of gaslights
   Show the towns from rim to rim,
While the leaden arch of twilight
   Spans the hill from brim to brim.

Spans the great tumultuous city
   Like an eagle wild with life,
Wings unfurled with winds of commerce,
   Every pinion plumed for strife.

Like an Apocalyptic vision
  Shone to illuminate the stones,
In a twinkling blazed the spirit
  Of the great electric suns.

In this grand illumination,
  Like a spirit climbed the moon
Down the side of Auburn, farther,
  The Charles River glowed like noon.

In that dawn of peace men pray for
  Looked the evening world—I thought
The grim batteries in the harbor
  Vanished then, like spectres swart.

Steely bands along the horizon
  Trace the waters of the bay,
Dipping downward into ocean
  Where its shores at sunrise lay.

Holy praises clearly musical
  Down the ambient air descend,
While the sickle slowly faded,
  As, the tombs were going to rend—

Sweeter sing those heavenly voices
  Praising over the graves of men,
And I saw the Seers and Poets
  Walking on the earth again.
November 2, 1883.

THE MARCH OF TIME.

1884.

Scarce had the angels' voices hushed
    Their song of " Peace to man,"
When all the galaxy of stars
    Another song began ;

Like Cherubim and Seraphim
    Around the Throne of Light,
They struck their golden harps, and Heaven
    Flashed with their music bright ;

Far in the Eastern Hemisphere
    Came rolling on the strains,
Sublime and sweet, as Thales heard
    On the Nilotic plains ;

Echo on echo touched the hills
    Which bursted into flame—
As the Parsee hailed the rising sun ;
    And Time passed on the same ;

Olympus summoned forth the Greeks
    To try the State's pastimes ;
And by " Olympiad " time was called
    In histories and in rhymes ;

'Folding his eagle wings awhile
  Upon Italia's plains;
From mighty " Roma "—was the date.
  Which long with time remains;

And thus passed down, the march of time;
  As men by time were schooled;
When time made conquest of them all
  As each one rose and ruled.

Scarce had the angels' voices hushed
  Their songs of " Love to man,"
When all the galaxy of stars
  Another song began;

For time upon his annual flight,
  Pausing on Bethlehem's plain
And listening to the angel's song,
  Joined with a new refrain;

Tender and sweet and like a bell
  It struck upon the ear,
The Wise men pause—to catch the note—
  Lifting the heart in prayer;

And Mary clasped her Holy born
  Listening to the strain;
For Time then, struck his harp but—" Once!"
  And then passed on again.

Within the palace, Herod clad
  In royal robes, had met

The Maji who had read the stars,
    Whose anxious faces set

The king's heart very ill at ease,
    Casting the fate which traced
An obscure King for Israel,
    By name " Messiah" graced ;

And time upon his annual round,
    Had heard the wailing cry
Of Israel's maids and mothers,
    For " Israel's babes should die ; "

Alighting upon Judea's plain
    And striking his harp—" Twice,"
It was the Christian—Century
    Which Time had made his prize.

If constant stars ring out a year
    And ring one in again,
Above their silvery twinklings, clear
    Is heard Old Time's refrain ;

Striking his harp on England's coast,
    By the stiff Eastern breeze
Its Sixteen Hundred notes were borne
    Over the Western seas ;

The Northern pine was ready strung
    With all its thousand strings ;

The Southern cypress heard its moss
   Like Jubal's harp—that sings;

And like a Spirit, with the ship,
   The Mayflower reached the dock,
And since, we've always counted time
   Dated from Plymouth Rock.

Scarce had the angels' voices hushed
   Their song of " Love to man,"
When all the galaxy of stars
   Another song began ;

Like Cherubim and Seraphim
   Around the Throne of Light;
They struck their golden harps, and Heaven
   Flashed with their music bright ;

Again, Old Time folds up his wings
   When all the fields are white,
A wreath of pine upon his brow,
   His sandals soft and light;

Again, he strikes his golden harp
   Under the midnight stars ;
Singing of Springtime, and the flowers
   Which at October pause ;

The roses die, the lilies fade,
   The leaves and fruits all go,

He's singing of these,--and the dead
    Under the snow below;

He sings of all life's gladdening hopes
    The New Year has in store,
While he is striking on his harp
    For Eighteen-Eighty-Four.

"Praise God from whom all blessings flow,
    Praise Him all creatures here below,
Praise Him above, ye heavenly host,
    Praise Father, Son, and Holy Ghost."

O YE HILLS.

O ye hills! O ye hills! when ye wake and rejoice
Like a great congregation ye lift up one voice;
When the Spirit of Light flieth over at morn,
And the stars at the rush of his wings are withdrawn;
Like the brightness that filled the Lord's house on the
    hill,
When the priests, for, the glow of Jehovah stood still,—
When the glory is streaming your arches along,
When your choirs of a thousand are full of their song,
When the incense goes up from the river and rill
Ye have both the old grandeur of temple and hill.

Ye are volumes of Time! upon every page
Of creation, you open the stories of age;

With the dove, that went forth at the lull of the flood,
When above the bare waters, old Ararat stood ;—

We see one displaying the banner of cloud
When the Law-giver opened his pleadings aloud,
And his commands went forth with the pledge of the
    Lord
"That the deeds of mankind should be judged by his
    word ; "

One is wrapped in a pall of great sorrow, so black,
The sun in the folds, lost its heavenly track,
The rocks moved about at the sob of the earth,—
The graves opened wide for the dead to come forth ;

Then the touch of the feet of a Christ upon one
The place was transfigured, with angels, thereon,
And lifting the vail He had worn among men
He revealed the Redeemer in heaven again.

Though ye pause on the way to the skies—ye are
    nearer,—
When altars were builded and heaven seemed clearer,
When the vintage empurpled to empty its wine,
When the olive was greened to a shading divine,
When the corn bowèd down to the earth and adored,
And they numbered the flocks, while Pans' harmony
    poured.

Ye were clad in the green robe of Peace !
                      But O Hills !
Ye have trenched on the Pride, and the Avarice that kills,

Ye have portioned the earth with your columnar walls,
And men looked on your face, were content—till the
　　calls
Of Ambition, unfurled them, its death dealing wings,
And the mountains were scaled, like the lowlier things,
And your ponderous gates were unlocked with the
　　sword :
But O God, the new earth has revealèd thy word,
For we go up like those who went singing a song,
Where the steam-driven chariot goes whirling along.

Ye are mightier than Cheops! ye are tombs of a race,—
Without groan, without pain, ye were reared into place,
And the red-men went free as the deer on the hill,
The proud men who were kinged with the bald-eagle's
　　quill,
Who told over the fall, summer, winter, and May,
From the planting of corn to the great hunting day
By the silvery lettering they read on the moon,
And the Great Spirit led them by sight as a boon,
And they hallowed the graves of their father's with love,
And rejoiced in the hunt and the bison above,
And with bow, and with arrow they went to the field
To themselves and their children, eternally sealed.

Ye are tombs of a race—but the type on your page
Is to dim, to discover the people or age !
Ye are tombs, ye are temples, ye are altars, ye are hills
Which the praise of Elohim—everlastingly fills,
And my heart breaketh up into song at your voice,
All that's in me hath joined your grand choir to rejoice.

DANIEL BOONE.

A REMINISCENCE.

IN the spring of 1855, after spending a night at the Capitol Hotel, Frankfort, Ky., we arose early the next morning to visit the cemetery before our departure by train. Climbing the foot-way which leads to the place, we found ourselves suspended some two hundred feet in the air upon the almost perpendicular face of the ascent, the path about eighteen inches wide, and rocks fringed with evergreens towering in magnificent height above our heads.

Resting at a point where a cool spring comes leaping down from its source and falls into a natural rock, we took in the scene with all the enthusiasm of a young traveler. The Kentucky river, with its bold, bastioned bluffs, was on our right; South Frankfort lay before us; the railroad at our feet; woods pressing close up to the track, and spreading away in umbrageous concourse, made up one of those romantic views we never forget.

Reaching the little wooden gate, we passed into the grounds and began our wanderings among the homes of the dead. We came at length upon a dimple in the land about twenty feet in diameter, where lay two graves, unmarked save by a number of cedar stumps, which had been lifted by the roots, trimmed a little and hauled to the place. On expressing our astonishment at the proximity of such rude monuments, our companion informed us that we were standing at the graves of Daniel Boone and his wife. We sat down on the sward overcome by the incident, and burying our faces in our hands, shed tears, and tried to recall what we had gathered in childhood from Flint's memoir of the wonderful hunter of Kentucky. We saw him now as he tridded the canebrake, and skulked through the forest to elude the wary Indian; we saw him as his eagle eye pierced the coverts which sheltered the game, or gleamed admiringly over some everglade of flowers, comprehending at a glance the hunter's paradise; and we wept at the dangers he had run and the foes he had encountered.

A hunter without a bow and a lover of nature, but most of all, of this nobleman of the wildwoods of our adopted state, we had chanced upon his resting place, were standing on the smallest spot of land he ever owned, were at the grave of Daniel Boone. Gathering a few splinters from the stumps as a memorial, we sorrowfully left the spot

and returned to the city, which has since erected a handsome monu-
ment, sculptured and chased with designs expressive of the pioneer's
experience; reflecting that in our homes of peace and comfort we can
never be too grateful or too faithful to the memory of the white braves
of early times. Boone died in 1818.

NATURE'S green casket here embalms
　　The sturdy pioneer,
And has arrayed her floral charms
　　Thereon these sixty year,
And flushed and royal autumn's trace
　　In season has been here,
And knightly winter holds his place
　　Beside the sacred bier.

The winds that cross the Cumberland
　　Have found the Hunter's grave,
And marked his repose on the strand
　　Of the blue Kentucky's wave,
The rich insculptured pile of men
　　Who reverently here trod,
Bespeak the culture, that has been
　　Reared from the savage sod.

Methinks the hero only lies
　　Alert, to meet the foe,
The stealthiest Indian feels his eyes—
　　Ere his rifle's flash can show,
He feels the ambush must reveal
　　A hunter of Kentucky,
Whose pale-faced bravery won the seal
　　For the ground so dark and bloody.

The noble forest-born, he wore
  Its freedom like a king,—
The trees umbrageous shades did pour
  And flowers thickly spring,
And beauteous nimble-footed deer
  Here roamed the hills and vales,
The newest, best primeval, here
  His sure birthright entails.

Wild-bred with Nature, he was as
  The pattern of our race,
Enjoyed her solitudes, but was
  Full of all human grace,
Partook of woman's sweetest love,
  And friendship's tenderest thrill,
All soft affections helped to move
  His strong, untutored will.

'Twas no silken fraternal bond
  That made men brothers then;
'Twas sacrifice, Godlike, and fond,
  As His who died for men;
Where the stockaded fort arose—
  For the emigrant's defense,
Was death shared like a boon by those
  Who scorned all self-defense.

Together sweetly sing the names
  Of Harold, Boone, and Kenton,
Around their valorous deeds there flames
  The Muse's noble mention,

Like them—she loves the generous West
    Who gives her here a portion,
But more, each bullet-proven breast
    Who gave it their devotion.

She plucks her pinion just to trace
    The Pioneer's bier,
And bows above his marble face
    To dew it with a tear,
It falls upon the turf that's green
    Above his restful bed,
And where the springing shaft is seen
    Her poetic bay has spread.

The morning's azure gates were spread,
    The rosy winds passed through,
A soft and golden splendor led
    Up each solemn avenue,
It walked as 't were the spirit of God,
    It found us there alone—
And, lo! we stood upon the sod,
    At the grave of Daniel Boone.

ENGLAND WILL CARE FOR EGYPT.

ENGLAND will care for Egypt, now she's old
    And tottering helpless, under her crown of stone;
When earth was fresh, with its primeval mold
    Her Asian founders, worshipers of the Sun,

Commenced her greatness, pride, longevity, glory,—
On her stone age immortalized their story.

England will care for Egypt, for her gods
　　Were, ages past, too feeble to help her people ;
And they have petrified beneath the floods
　　Of sands which drowned them, and the great upheaval
Of Nilus brings no devotee to prayer,—
The mysteries of Osiris are laid bare.

England will care for Egypt as a kingdom,
　　Not th' aristocratic beggar of a Porte ;—
This mother of nations is the Eastern Bedlam
　　Her laws a pest, her revolutions sport ;
And here the Pharaohs swayed, the Ptolemies fell,
The Mamelukes murdered—Arabi died as well.

England will care for Egypt and her tradition,
　　Zoan's groaning stones, heard in their glyphic traces,
While scholars are using the torch of erudition
　　Peering into the rock imprisoning Ramases,
The Hebrew host, the march, the route they fled
Not alone in the Myth of Papyrus, are read.

England will care for Egypt till her stones
　　Have sung and spoken and groaned out all they know ;
Her hieroglyphics like her Ra-faced suns
　　And her fructifying Osiris set aflow
Thousands of living streams of sacred truth
Her monuments have pent up in her youth.

Till men who felt her darkness, see her truth
  Now hewing it through, as the Egyptian fog
Was broken and lifted—when the Hebrews' ruth
  Had driven them to their Exodus, and the bog
Sibornian passed, the sea drank up their foes;
  Egypt's stone volumes, tell us what she knows.
  February, 1884.

THE CHRISTMAS SNOW-STORM.

[With a Temperance Moral.]

THE shoulders of the clouds, at last
Tired of their fleece of snow,
Casting it to the winds to bear
Away to earth below,
Though wound around their grasping fists
To carry safely down,
The fringes caught upon the hills
And chimneys of the town,
Snapping it loudly as they flew,
The forest bare they passed
And left some hanging, like the sails
Upon a navy's mast,
Clutching the rest with fingers stiff
They soar, they dip, they leap,
The rocky ledge tears off some shreds
Which they roll in a heap,
Tossing the balls with airy feet
Into the fields below
Like children at their winter sport

Of tumbling in the snow;
Again, inflated like a puff
And rolling round the sky
'Twas caught up in the stubborn knots
Only the winds can tie,
'Twas like a pendulum all day
Swinging from left to right,
But now—it lay in cloggy drifts
As dropped the winds with night,
The bearings of the road were lost
Over the stretch between
The city and the farm-house, where
My actors can be seen.

"John, bring a back-log from the pile
Of the fall hickory
You cut in the October days
The best stick of the tree!
And, while you're out, just shut the cows
Into the southern shed,
And with the corn and salted hay
The herd must be well fed!
And from the mow throw down a bed
For Filly, Sweet, and Roan,
To beasts, on such a night as this
Man's best side may be shown!
In weather such as this, I wish
My house and barns were great
Enough, to shelter many more
Till the dreadful cold abate;
I never eat our bread, but what

I think of some who would
Do more work, in the Master's cause,
And do His name more good;
My bins are filled, until they look
As if their waists must ache,
I must put all my substance by,—
I can no field forsake,—
But such a spell as this—I wish
I could fulfill God's word—
Send for the poor in His by-ways
To come and share my board;
My Bible tells me what to do,
It's friendly to the poor,
John! put the back-log on, and set
The chimney in a roar
Letting the glow across the snow
Point some one to our door;
The sheep were in the fold all day,
See they are all secure!
The flock in such a night as this
If sheltered, may endure,
The rooster and his wives will keep
Their perch, while this will stay,
And so escape the stiff'ning cold
Tucked in the loft away."

"Yes, Ezra, we have tried to live
By christian love contently,
The kind that's practiced with the lips
Don't always touch one's plenty,
And when I heard the hum and whir

Of Maggie's wheel all day,
I thought of all the smiles I'd get
For what I'd give away.
You know our neighbor Brimful's left
His children in the cold,
To see how much money, the till
Of old Pint's shop can hold,—
His Belle has got no gown to wear
To church, and stays at home
Because, he helped to buy the furs
For Pint's Sue, who can come,—
The boys, can wear their Kerseymere
And boots which cost a ten,
For Brimful will go there and drink
His whisky with the men;
O, I remember what was said
When his Robert went away,
The coals heaped then, upon his heart,
Would burn as deep to-day
And daily burned the wound—it made
In the boy's soul, to put
The scanty earnings in Pint's till,
Though his poor lips were mute;—
I sent John o'er at early morn
With socks and milk and meal,
The woman is too weak to work,
Pint's shame she can't conceal,
But with her fragile life she'll cling
Unto her children more,
She's but a broken-hearted thing
With hope turned from the door.

" Maggie, your fingers were so deft
    Spinning the rolls to-day,
Just stop drawing the thread awhile
    And put the wheel away,
And take the half-peck apple tray
    And bring it heaping full,
And soon we'll have some toasting hot
    Roasting before the yule.

" 'Ten years ago to-night, Ezra,
    If you'll think so far back—
Our William put his worldly all
    Into a little pack,
Talking in such a strain, the while,
    And I thought boyish-wise
About the wond'rous steps and turns
    Which up to Fortune rise,
About another kind of stock
    Which takes a premium,
'Of gold and silver and per cent
    Until my lips grew dumb,
So rich and gaudy—till I thought
    The fire-dogs stared at me
Leering their eyes far back, to sneer
    Up at our plain roof-tree ;
I brought the Bible from the drawers
    And laid it on the stand,
To prove the filial chain was strong
    He gave us each a hand,
And then you read in Matthew, two,
    'The Bethlehem babe was born,'—

Our own came on a Christmas eve
We named it ' Will,' next morn ;
I thought of him so much to-day
Since John brought home the pine,—
He was our angel, sent us in
The place of one divine,—
I often wonder at the joy
Which followed him—we've known
Such stores of comfort, since that day,
Ourselves, and in our own."

" Yes, mother, I have watched the snow
Like frightened birds, all day
Come dropping down the air in flocks
Or blown by winds away,
And when the fields were bleak with white
A host of graves were seen,
For every stump and shrub were like
A stone where one had been ;
So gloomy are my thoughts, for I
Keep thinking of the boy,
I fear his visit is postponed
And so, with it, our joy,
But, Maggie, give the fire a poke
And turn the apples round,
The room shall wear the welcome look,
As our joy-hour was found !
You tell the story o'er so true,
I see it now before
My eyes, as though that year did not
Run backward half a score,

Go place the bible on the stand
I'll read the chapter two,
There's something dim before my eyes—
Won't let the letters show,—
The cold must have searched out my chest,—
My voice is growing worse,—
Do mother, take your specks and read—
The rest from the sixth verse.—

"Hark! John go out to the front door
I thought I heard a ring,
A cutter might come out from town
Now it has stopped snowing!
The station's but three miles away
And if the boy has come,
He'll never mind the drifts, that lie
Between there and his home!"

"By Jingo! Mr. Warren come
And bring the light straight-way,
I think they got the engine bell
And hitched it to the sleigh!
That horse has on a head of steam—
And if they do n't break up
Before this house, the runners won't
Follow long behind his croup!
The snap that's in the man who can
Turn this frost, would suffice
The weather-clerk to put into
His batch of winter's ice!
Je-mi-ma! he's run on the switch

THE CHRISTMAS SNOW-STORM. 137

And brought up, at the gate,
I 'm out to tell the stranger, where,
They best accommodate!
Steady, and let the light's sliver
Shine straight across the snow,
Your hope is like a prophecy
I think it has brought two!"

"William, my boy, I see that we
Still the Lord's favor gain,
The years pass on, and leave us old,
They do not leave us pain
Since you come home each Christmas Eve
And make us young again."

"Well, father, bid the stranger in
And have him share your fire,
Together we left town at morn,
Through snow the train did mire,—
Beside, I'm his best, faithful friend,
And he has heard enough
Of farmer Warren's heavenly side
To try his earthly stuff."

"Bless me; I think I look into
Young Robert Brimful's face;
The beard has grown upon his chin—
But my dim sight can trace
The speaking truth still in his eyes,
Nobleness across his brow,
While chestnut curls still cluster round
His head in many a row,

This Christmas storm has favoring gales
For neighbor Brimful's sail,
The Lord has blessings in reserve,
I see, for those who fail."

CAPTAIN JOHN J. DESMOND,

A VICTIM OF THE RIOT, CINCINNATI, MARCH 29, 1884.

SUGGESTED by the pathetic wail of his distracted mother—"Oh that
he had been a coward."

WHY that wail of despair which to heaven did fly?
The hero had conquered his march to the bier,
He had died like a soldier, as men love to die
When the call has been just and the duty severe,
As men answer the call when their country's assailed
By invaders abroad or by tyrants at home,
When the Laws are defied and Injustice entailed
And the growl can be heard, of the Avenger to come.

'Twas a woman who uttered that wail of despair,
A mother, who saw that a bullet had crashed
Through the brain of a son she had cultured with care,
While she held every foe to his honor abashed.
On her gray hairs has fallen the glow of his name,
With its honor maintained, he could strive for a crown,
On her brow too, has fallen the rays of his fame,
He was twining the wreath which would bring him re-
          nown.

'Twas the wail of a mother, who knew that her boy
Had been torn from the breasts which had fed him with
    milk,
Had been snatched from the lips which had kissed his
    with joy,
From the hands which caressed his small fingers of
    silk ;
She could wail for her babe without weakness or fear,
Not with precept of courage, with the precept of Love
She had conquered his heart,—as the sunbeams appear
To attract and dissolve every storm-cloud above.

Did she wail o'er a hero? then she wailed o'er a son !
She had taught him " forgiveness is stronger than war,
That a kiss for a blow is not cowardly done,
Cowards likewise are braver, than breakers of Law ; "
There's no shadow can tarnish the gold of his name,
To the grave, it will carry her gray hairs in peace,
There's no leaf to be clipped from the wreath of his
    fame,
For the Right, do the crowns, of the martyrs increase.

THE PITIFUL SIGHT OF THE CHANGING
YEAR.

THE winds are cracking their gusty whips
And surrying through the sky,
As they were driving the flocks of snow
Which in the Northward fly,

The forests mourning in suits of black,
The earth is wrinkled and old,
　　But the pitiful sight of the changing year
　　Is the poor hungry and cold.

What earthly joy have the very poor?
What comfort or what content
In a rickety house with a broken roof,
When the bitterest blasts are sent?
When the cold creeps over their trembling limbs
In a stiff"ning and snaky fold?
　　O the pitiful sight of the changing year
　　Is the poor hungry and cold.

A handful of fire on the broken hearth,
A smothering, smoking pile
He blows, with a remnant of feeble breath
That a spark of hope may smile,
A pittance of coal from the frozen street
Which the rich man's ashes hold,
　　O the pitiful sight of the changing year
　　Is the poor hungry and cold.

Why need the poor a well-filled shed
When the cellar is empty and bare?
The harvest of summer seems not for him,
Though the Lord sent enough and to spare;
" Where there's little of food, there's little of fire "
Is the shortest sermon told,
　　O the pitiful sight of the changing year
　　Is the poor hungry and cold.

The preacher may call till the day of doom
On the wicked to "be saved,"
The prison will gape wide as the church
When men are by want enslaved,
There were never fetters forged so sure,
Or bolts that so surely hold,
    O the pitiful sight of the changing year
    Is the poor hungry and cold.

There was never a fiend like the fiend of want,
There was never a curse like this,
The body can sin, and the soul feel pure—
As an angel up in bliss,
While man is judging the outward act,
His God does the inward hold,
    O the pitiful sight of the changing year
    Is the poor hungry and cold.

O God has cheapened His stores, that man
Shall have no want to bear,
The North and the South have filled the land
With abundance to eat and to wear,
Yet thousands seek for work in vain,
Eating the bread that's doled,
    O the pitiful sight of the changing year
    Is the poor hungry and cold.

THE ROSE.

THERE is something divine in your marvelous grace
That tells where the Spirit of Love must abide,
While the blushes of modesty seen on your face
Preserves from a touch of the Spirit of Pride.

Ye meet at the bridal, where mirthfulness lends
Like the cloy of a passion, a sadness of voice,
On your splendor the thorn of the Spirit attends,
While the heart on your odorous balm will rejoice.

In your beauty ye gather to cover the bier,
With a radiance dispelling the thought of relief,
The features of death in your presence appear
Too lovely for earth and too holy for grief.

Ye are twined for the bugle, the banner, the arch,
Where the feet of the conqueror proudly will tread,
In the stains of their glory, the victors will march
To stain with your beauty, the graves of their dead.

Ye are gayest, to meet where the dancers convene,
Where Joy swoons and revives in the music's bright
        power,
Though the fires of love rival your tropical sheen,
Fond bosoms are clasped by your love-knots this hour.

With our Passion ye meet, from the crib to the bier,
Still uncloyed, are expecting your beautiful bloom
Where a heaven will wipe from our face every tear,
And its June in the flame of its Roses consume.

SWEET SPIRIT OF LOVE.

SWEET Spirit of Love, can'st thou prolong
   This ecstasy of love an hour?
Confessions, which to thee belong
   Give me supremely, to thy power,
But thou can'st bring me no repose
   When once the fickle thrill awakes,
The heart it enters, ne'er can close,
   Its ecstasy subdues or breaks.

I open all my heart and fling
   Upon thy bosom all that's told,
Thou sweet intoxicant, and cling
   As mad,—yet thou did'st break my hold,
And Earth has lost its paradise
   And heart-communion lost its bliss
Because that hour forever flies
   When every vein was thrilled with this.

Sweet Spirit of Love, if there's a place
   Where thou eternally can'st stay,
And not be driven in disgrace
   Into the realms of outer day,

Perhaps, to find the men, there, gods,
　　To find the women, angels,—where
So e'er the place, love makes no odds
　　Betwixt courtship and marrying there.

———

LOVE AFTER TEA.

I.

How bright are the pictures which young recollection
Throws onto the foreground of life as we pass,
But truer and fonder, in those hours of reflection
When husband and wife hold the magical glass.
While pencils of bright flame are etching the lamp
　　　　white
Whose mellowing glow fills the room every-where,
Enjoying their rockers drawn close to the fire-light
Two faces are clearing of wrinkles and care.

II.

Her swift flying feet have been ready to answer
The constant exactions of pleasure and pain,
Her fingers though skillful will never advance her
Beyond what to-day has done over again,—
The odds and the ends for the household all finished,
The maid of all work left with nothing to do,
The children at last, leave the circle diminished,
Alone, at the fire-side the lovers are two.

III.

Her eyes kindly twinkle with love for the husband,
The smiles brightly mist o'er his beard for the wife,
The tick of the second goes teasing the hour-hand
And no longer troubling the passage of life,—
Two hearts beat as one in the purest communion
That comes, after seal of connubial ban,
And lips meet to kiss in the holiest union,
The kiss that is shameless 'twixt woman and man.

IV.

And there, as two angels sat down 'mong the lilies
Where whitest and sweetest in heaven above,
Beatified ones, by the blessèd affinities
Of love, in the spirit of all that is love,
Their troubles all cast on the Healing Physician,
Again there are two, in the Eden of man,
The tempter has slunk to the shades of perdition
And love shows divine, in the conjugal plan.

    FALL RIVER, MASS., *July* 28, 1883.

MAMMOTH CAVE.

THE first verse of the poem was composed at the cave; the remain-
der in the stage-coach on the way to Cave City, ten miles distant.

WHEN earth terraqueous left the Creator's hand,
Water contended with the encroaching land;
And a diluvial ocean in its flow
Carried the cunning lime unto its foe,

Which storing up the bottom of the sea
The lime-rock there was born; as God, would be,
Using the forces of the rebellious wave
To build the dungeons of the Mammoth Cave.

Honored by God with an eternal age,
Man feels His awful presence on each page;
Hears how His mighty spirit moves the sea;
The firmaments round out immensity;
And dense with darkness, earth has seen no light
Under thick clouds which shut the heaven from sight,
When the young world rose dripping from the wave
Which piled the bed-rock of the Mammoth Cave.

The sun was ladened with its gaseous breath,
And all the atmosphere was filled with death;
Except, the rocks, nature had swooned away,—
Beauty had found no medium for its ray,—
Gigantic forests slumbered in the germ
Ferns and club-mosses, till their awakening term,
And the subsidence of the acidulous wave
Which cut the rock-ribs of the Mammoth Cave.

Now like the rush of angels' wings, the breeze
Sung its first lullaby across the seas;
The earth beheld the splendor of the bow
Spanning the heaven—where gods are said to go,
And well they might, and not dishonor Him
Who makes the glory of the angels dim;
And sparkling with the beauty of the wave,
The rock had blossomed, in the Mammoth Cave.

True to the rule of Time, which gives the crown
After the trial of the cross is borne,
God hung the rose upon the cavern's mouth,
The violet put her jacinth petals forth
And drank the dew, when still condensing night
Had cooled the earth and vapor floating light,
And Light had kissed as fondly drop and wave
And made its covenant with the Mammoth Cave.

O crown of mind, O Immortality,
Go find the forces of the land and sea!
Explore the heaven and earth, and thou shalt see
God will be God of all their mystery!
Yield up thy pride, " to look upon His face,"
And take thy life a favor of His grace,
For thou shalt bow before Him, like the wave
Which built the caverns of the Mammoth Cave.
August 9, 1882

A SCRAP OF POETRY.

NOGAMOTO O. KABE, a Japanese prince, completed his studies at Yale College; made the tour of the United States and Europe, returning to Japan in 1883.

THANK Heaven, it is one song fills all the Earth,
Sung in the same language, in the same chord of music,
Terrestrially, in all souls it has birth,
Celestially, it is the song cherubic.

Love, Brotherhood, Humanity are one,
One magnetism finds in all a power,

Where Asian Islands first induce the Sun
To mould his splendor into fruit and flower,

Where torrid Afric rears the tower of palm,
Where Ocean keeps the chains of Arctic on,
Where Earth needs vassals, and mankind need balm,
Love does translate all languages—by one.

Here's every zone, here every race can flourish,
Here every product grows and vegetates,
With all we are Republican, we nourish
All men with freedom, knowledge, and estates.

In that dear Isle Nippón, O then recall
The awaiting for you in this "Home sweet home,"
Your lines in pleasant places here did fall,
Old Yale's your *Mater*, wheresoe'er you roam.

———

THE PIPE OF PEACE.

PRESIDENT HAYES was presented with the Peace-Pipe, Sept. 28, 1877.

A BARBARIC bowl is the Indian's pipe,
  The sacred Pipe of Peace ;
'Tis hewn from the old rock's flinty grip,
Then hollowéd out, for its roomy lip,
  And carved with the bison's fleece
And antlers grasping each spiny tip
  Round the Indian Pipe of Peace.

A reed of slender stem they wind
  With plumes—which the eagle frees,
And filled with weed, where'er they find
The spirit of good in the human kind
  They light the Pipe of Peace,
The lips of the Indian when combined
  Bring forth the spirit of peace.

It has written like ink the silvery air,
  The smoke of the Pipe of Peace ;
A treaty of peace by the blue Delaware
When the father of love the Lennäppé met there
  And he purchased the lands of these,
The oath of the red-man was sacred who sware
  With Penn on the Pipe of Peace.

It has sweeten'd the lips of the brave Illinois
  The breath of the Pipe of Peace;
When the priest of the white man accepted his toy,
The breast of the savage was throbbing with joy
  After smoking the Pipe of Peace,
The Christ of Marquette, was a vision t'enjoy,
  He saw in the Pipe of Peace.

It has banded a brotherhood distant and wide
  The smoke of the Pipe of Peace ;
It has glisten'd with spray from the Ocean tide,
Has rolled like a cloud up the Cumberland side
  And swung o'er Yosemite's
And sprung like the elk 'cross the Great Divide
  The smoke of the Pipe of Peace.

If the white man carries a selfish heart
    When he smokes the Pipe of Peace,
From their lands and their homes they must depart—
O the Cherokee knoweth the graves apart
    Of his Braves—he left with these—
From his graves condemn'd, since taking the part
    Of pariah, the whites to please.

If the Choctaw lived like the white brave, when
    He offered the Pipe of Peace,
The laws of the whites, were the laws of men
Who conquer'd a world, were conquering then
    Every foot of ground from these,
They too must depart to be savages, when
    The white Brave was to please.

Yes, the white men carry a selfish heart
    When they smoke the Pipe of Peace;
Though the hills were of gold, it was their part
To do, as they'd wish the Indian heart
    Would do by them, with these,
O Red Cloud found the cross—his part
    Of the white men's vision of peace.

The White Father, only had this to tell,
    When he smoked the Pipe of Peace;
"The rivers are numbered by which they dwell,
Th' forests are numbered and numbers foretell
    The last of the Pipes of Peace.
For Nature has claims, she must yield as well
    And the braves must yield with these."

THE DANDELION.

CROWN me with Dandelion
  Strewn by the Spring,
Full of the cheery gold
  Found in a ring,
Full of the maiden-breath
  Found in a flower,
Bring me the starry-gold
  Fresh, to my bower.

After the feet of the
  Spring have flown by,
Leaving the field like
  A patch of the sky,
Down, 'mong the grasses
  They twinkle and shine,
She's the enchantress
  Who opens the mine.

Rich, as the yellow coin
  Made at the mint,
With the sweet face of spring
  For the imprint,
Gather the starry-gold
  Rich as a Jew's—
For the bright buckles too,
  Worn on my shoes.

THE NORTHMEN.

O THEY are gallant, gallant Captains
   Who sail to the Polar Main,
To conquer by courage and not by sword
   The cold on its native plain.

Who gallantly, gallantly drive their ships
   Into the icebergs' jaws,
And woe to the crew and the navy too
   When caught in their bloodless maws.

They have gallant, gallant hearts who wait
   While the Sun is held at bay,
And Cold and Darkness six long months
   Hold stern titanic sway.

They have gallant, gallant spirits who watch
   The fight six months prolong,
When the Sun enforces his titan sway
   And the cold reinforced too strong.

As gallant a Dutchman as ever has sailed
   His frigate away to the North
Where ice grows faster than corn at the South,
   Was Heemskerk with the pluck of his cloth.

As gallant a crew as from England sailed
   Was charmed by the Kraken cold,

Were crushed in its toils—like the Laocoön,
    With no grave but its icy fold.

As gallant, as gallant as admiral could be
    And brave as a lion for its cub,
McClintock quadrupled his search for Sir John
    As though the North Pole he would snub.

And Kane has twice entered the den of the bear
    And twice herbinated in ice,
And Hall took meridians and parallels there
    While the icicles froze to his eyes.

And Nordenskold gallantly circled the Pole
    And came through the East by a door
That never was opened because of the cold
    By any bold sailor before.

As gallantly Schwatka did hazard his life
    Where Franklin and Irving remain,
Where Cheops in ice, will immortalize fame
    And the cold will as deathless complain.

Far, far more eternal than marble or bronze
    These tablets their valor enroll,
No sound of the hammer and graver is heard
    In building their tombs at the Pole.

The valorous men who tried bearding the cold,—
    DeLong who succumbed to its spies,
Danenhower's ursine grip on the fiend of the Pole,
    Greely's rescue from famine and ice,

Where Seehley as gallantly, gallantly went
　When the dying a paladin call,
This frigid sea-errantry calls for a man
　To be offered up Christlike for all.

Wilks, D'Unville and Ross, with those gallant com-
　· mands
　Who felt the ice crunching their bones,
O as gallant commands as ever nations sent
　Have sailed to the frozen zones.

THE SLAVE'S PURCHASE.

FREEDOM that's purchased with Slavery, must be
Freedom the sweetest descended from Liberty;
For Time which appears to grow like any tree
Seems ever increasing, buying it, to be free;
And Hope that glitters on the distant goal, a star,
Oftentimes must sink too low to shine,—at war
With that emotional gloominess in the soul
When high the billows of desperation roll—
And nigh to drowning in this abandonment, he
Discovers no Saving Rock but Slavery,
No hope but in bondage, kissing even this rod,
But feeling a grave under every foot of sod;
O what rewards shall Heaven award the slave
Who himself raised—body, soul, mind—from such
　grave?

And when his lungs are inflated with freedom, he
Bondage assumes, till he buys wife and children **free**;
O man is love in Liberty like this?
Would'st thine toil, suffer, sacrifice like his?
Patriots will die for country, moralists die
For principle, and Christians die for faith.
And men have died for men in Slavery,—
But not like the freedman treading the wheel to **save**
The souls which see no ultimate but a grave;
Who will define such love as his?   A wraith
Comes in love's place after death or separation,—
Yet this man toils, will make grander abnegation
For love which the master would destroy, than he
Who owns the slave and holds all love is free;
Such love among the freedmen proves to me
That hearts have broken of love in Slavery!
O what rewards will Heaven award the slave
Who raised his wife and children from this grave?
O Freedom that's purchased with slavery, must be
Freedom the sweetest descended from **Liberty**!

    KENTUCKY, *September* 1, 1884.

CENTENNIAL SONGS.

THE following Centennial songs were published in brochure during 1876, in Peoria, Ills.

Inspired with the sentiments of a patriot and the principles of a Unionist, a grave reverence for the solemn responsibilities assumed by our early fathers in fighting and conquering for us this sacred trust, and the prayerful hope that statesmen will conscientiously protect and advance the high interest confided to their keeping, the authoress must wish, that all who read these songs could be likewise inspired with the love of that freedom which

"Utters thunder till the world shall cease."

SONG OF THE TEA KETTLE.

AIR.—Home, Sweet Home.

HARK to the song which the tea-kettle sings,
  The domestic tea-kettle, boiling for tea,
Clattering its lid—and at every puff flings
  A cloud, that grows fast, as a tempest at sea.
    "Home, Home, sweet, sweet home.
      There's no place like home, there's no place like
      home."

When the great man at home put his hand in his pocket
  And whined out so often, " he had n't a pound
To wager at piquet or swell the war docket,"
  What could the lords do then but give him more ground?
    " Home, Home, sweet, sweet home," etc.

Till all of the homes which their cousins did settle
  And bodies—and pockets—and consciences too

Belong to the king—who by warrants could nettle
  His subjects with the old yoke just furbished anew.
    " Home, Home, sweet, sweet home," etc.

And then when our forefathers had to send over
  A distance of three thousand miles for a hat
And crow-bar and paper,—they thought they could
    love her—
  But make these at home, as they 'd genius for that.
    " Home, Home, sweet, sweet home," etc.

Said England : " But O how maternal, to send them
  Their clothing and furnish their tables beside,
Perhaps they 'll cry out, ' its oppression, or our phlegm,'
  We 'll keep them a visiting, though, till they 've died! "
    " Home, Home, sweet, sweet home," etc.

" Their uncles, and aunties, and cousins, are striving
  At home here, to keep them supplied with enough,
Perhaps they 'll die too, of the trouble of living,
  If we do n't give the colonies shops a rebuff. "
    " Home, Home, sweet, sweet home," etc.

" We 'll tax them on sugar, and rum, and molasses,
  Forbid Carolina to make tar and staves,
We'll send them our wines too—and just to try passes—
  We 'll send o'er a cargo of tea, to the slaves. "
    " Home, Home, sweet, sweet home," etc.

The tea-kettle dried up its drops of vexation
  I thought all its vapors of hate, it had poured,

When suddenly hissing a splenetic " *taxation*,"
   I thought, 't was the night the tea went overboard.
     " Home, Home, sweet. sweet home," etc.

YANKEE DOODLE.

December 16—'73
   They gave the great tea party,
And when they got through with the tea
   The men were feeling hearty
     And everybody whistled then
       The tune of Yankee Doodle,
     It stirred up all the minute men ·
     And roused the British poodle.

They ban the courts to Salem-town,
   And shut the custom-houses
And Boston looks a little down,
   Before her spleen composes
     But everybody whistled then
       The tune of Yankee Doodle,
     It stirred up all the minute men
     And roused the British poodle.

It snarled, until it got a bill
   Through parliament to carry,
To quarter troops in Boston, till,
   The people they could harry
     And everybody whistled then
       The tune of Yankee Doodle,

It stirred up all the minute men
And roused the British poodle.

The ports deserted, customs stopped,
• Wharves waiting for the duster
You may have thought their courage dropped,—
They'd more than they dared muster
 For everybody whistled then
  The tune of Yankee Doodle,
 It stirred up all the minute men
  And roused the British poodle.

And when the British troops marched out
 Eight hundred strong, for Concord,
Eighty true patriots set about
 A rally to the good Lord
 And everybody whistled then
  The tune of Yankee Doodle,
 It cheered up all the minute men
  But roused the British poodle.

As times looked blue, the Whigs called for
 A Congress to assemble
Which showed a deadly sting for war,
 Making the British tremble
 And everybody whistled then
  The tune of Yankee Doodle,
 It cheered up all the minute men
  But roused the British poodle.

With thirteen rattles in its tail
 The Colonial snake prepared

To make th' British constrictor quail,
  To see its rights were squaréd
    And everybody whistled then
      The tune of Yankee Doodle,
    It stirred up all the minute men
      And roused the British poodle.

They showed what stuff they were made of
  As well as a flint musket,
At Bunker Hill they spilled enough
  Of blood to make the grass wet
    And everybody whistled then
      The tune of Yankee Doodle,
    It cheered up all the fighting men
      And roused the Britsh poodle.

And if they thought our brain was light
  And thought our heart conceity,
For Yankee Doodle we did fight
  Until we forced a treaty
    And everybody whistled then
      The tune of Yankee Doodle,
    Before the world we are the men
      Who whipped the British Poodle.

THE TRUMPET.

AIR.—"Portuguese Hymn."

THEN, like it rolled from the blast of a trumpet,
"O nation! I try every cause in a balance,

The Right shall weigh down, and the Wrong shall weigh
up,
One word of my fiat is more than your talents ;
Bare the sword ! let every man's right arm be
ready
And the foe shall melt down, like the foam on
the sea.

" Put on the whole armor, to go into battle !
'The cuirass of Truth, and the helmet of Justice,
The tough shield of Godliness, borne through the con-
flict
And the cause you fight for, shall go never amiss,
Bare the sword ! let every man's right arm be
ready
And the foe shall melt down, like the foam on
the sea.

" 'T is I, who have measured the girth of the oceans,
With continents fairest, their bosoms begemmed,
They sit there, like sisters, but one ye shall people
With races of freemen, which tyrants condemned,
Bare the sword ! let every man's right arm be
ready
And the foe shall melt down, like the foam on
the sea.

" They shall leave you alone, in the land that ye came to,
Your ships, was the rod that divided the sea,
Your cause has the pillar of fire in the night-time,
By day for your pillar of cloud I will be,

Bare the sword! let every man's right arm be
  ready
And the foe shall melt down, like the foam on
  the sea.

" Ye have taken a leader, a man I have chosen,
  Ye shall follow and fight where his valor leads you,
Armipotent he shall lead you out victorious,
  In my strength I have panoplied him to go through,
    Bare the sword! when every man's right arm is
      ready
The foe shall melt down, like the foam on the sea."

THE FLAG—JANUARY 1, 1876.

TUNE.—Red, White, and Blue.

It flies, it flies, is it a living thing?
  Did it come from out the sky?
Does it sail along on feathery wing?
  Is it angel, bird or fly?
It delights to fly in mountain air
  Which ripens the mountain grass,
It climbs from scrap to escarp there
  Where shocks of rude winds pass.

    God be with us where e'er we may be,
    Victory perch on the Flag of the Free!
    Proudly waving away War's red wraith,
    O'er our Freedom it hovers like Faith.

  It darts right toward the direst storm
  And where the lightnings lance

And where the thunders growl alarm
    Turns there, its eagle glance ;
It descends to the gentle gales
    That swing o'er plains below,
It comes!   On azure wing it sails
    With golden stars aglow.

      God be with us where e'er we may be,
      Victory perch on the Flag of the Free!
      Proudly waving away War's red wraith,
      O'er our Freedom it hovers like Faith.

It is, it is the bonny flag
    By young freemen unfurled,
Who swore a great oath ne'er to fag
    Till honored by the world ;
Who swore to try afield the appeal
    And met the vaunting foe,
And there with arms as true as steel
    To strike where it should go.

      God be with us where e'er we may be,
      Victory perch on the Flag of the Free!
      Proudly waving away War's red wraith,
      O'er our Freedom it hovers like Faith.

Who swore, where cannons boomed, to go
    Where'er their colors lead,
And where their rifles hissed, to show
    No foeman there could tread ;
Who swore to carry it where suns
    Were wiped from off the sky—

By smoke and flame, from raging guns
　That spat their wrath so high.

　　God be with us where e'er we may be,
　　Victory perch on the Flag of the Free!
　　Proudly waving away War's red wraith,
　　O'er our Freedom it hovers like Faith.

It snapped, defiance, like the wind—
　One hundred years ago,
When men united as one mind
　All hardships to forego;
Meeting the bristling front of war
　And 'mid its iron talk,
Did write in blood, a clause of law
　At Trenton, Guilford, York.

　　God be with us where e'er we may be,
　　Victory perch on the Flag of the Free!
　　Proudly waving away War's red wraith,
　　O'er our Freedom it hovers like Faith.

Though shattered on the Brandywine
　Under a leaden scourge,
It waved a defiant ensign
　O'er the camp at Valley Forge;
But shaking prouder every fold
　When kissed by the June sun,
At Monmouth where the victory rolled
　Our flag the fairest, shone.

　　God be with us where e'er we may be,
　　Victory perch on the Flag of the Free!

Proudly waving away War's red wraith,
O'er our Freedom it hovers like **Faith.**

The gales at sea might beat its bars
    And rain of fire pour hard
As when flying with all its scars
    From the Bonhomme Richard;
But life was in the bonny flag
    By young freemen unfurled,
Who swore a great oath ne'er to fag
    Till honored by the world.
      God be with us where e'er we may be,
      Victory perch on the Flag of the Free!
      Proudly waving away War's red wraith,
      O'er our Freedom it hovers like Faith.

AULD LANG SYNE.

O, countrymen, join all and sing
    " Our happy, happy land,"
Divided we are always weak,
    United we shall stand,
      We sing the songs we used to sing
        In good old days of yore,
      That forced to rove, the winds will waft
        Us to our native shore,
The good old songs we used to sing
    For good old days of yore,
That forced to rove, the winds will waft
    Us to our native shore.

Where'er to-day, our countrymen
  They'll recollect her fame,
And sing the songs we sing at home
  To celebrate her name,
    They'll sing the songs we used to sing
      In good old days of yore,   •
    That wafted back to native land
      Their hearts will rove no more,
The good old songs they love to sing
  For good old days of yore,
That wafted back to native land
  Their hearts shall rove no more.

May all who've left their kindred dear
  And made with us a home,
Find all the laws so pure and just
  They'll care no more to roam,
    Then join and sing the songs we sung
      In good old days of yore,
    That wafted here from fatherland,
      Your hearts may rove no more,
The good old songs we love to sing
  For good old days of yore,
That wafted here from fatherland
  Your hearts may rove no more.

INDEPENDENCE BELLS—1776–1876.

LET the reader of the Independence Bells reflect, that the tories of the Revolutionary war must have been as chagrined at the mention of the successes of the Continental army as any Confederate can be at the mention of battles won by the Union army. It is imbecile and wicked to ignore our nation's history. The battles for the Union will as surely be read for all time, as the battles of England, France, Germany, Spain, Italy, or the conflicts of Russia and the Turks.—[AUTHORESS.

THE OLD BELL.

" HARK ! to the Independence Bell
   From the dome of Liberty Hall !
The tale our iron lips can tell
   Like an old veteran's fall,
Come up and hear the story, 'mid
   The scenes of the olden time,
Where, our first throb for Freedom, did
   Set ringing every chime.

"Our pulse was beating just as strong
   As any in the town,
When feverish bullets sped along
   The plains of Lexington,
And when our stumbling foemen fell
   Into their open graves,
The red lettering they left could tell
   What deeds, the patriot braves.

" And when the swiftest couriers swoop
   Down, on the scattered towns,

And tell, how every British troop
  Deserts the Boston downs,
The bell it went off with a peal
  As sudden as a rocket!
Franklin's old printing-press did feel
  Also, the spirit of it!

" It was a hundred years ago
  We held our speechful tongue,
The sentient bell : waiting to show
  When the grandest deed was done ;
Just like a mighty angel would
  With trumpet at his mouth,
To roll a blast of tidings good
  O'er North, East, West, and South.

" What yearning, prayerful hearts were led
  Up to the throne that day :
That prayer for " Independence " said
  Enough, to give it sway,
And when the immortal names went on
  The parchment with the rod,
It was our new commandment stone
  Right from the hand of God.

" If Aaron's rod can bud and bear
  Long as his priesthood stands,—
That pen has dropped a seed on, there,
  That's growing to shade all lands,
A mighty tree, wherein the tribes
  Can shelter, just the tree

The olden, and prophetic scribes
　　Told, 'Jesus said, 't would be.'

" The eager patriots caught the sound
　　And learned how freedom spoke !
The tidal wave of joy it found,
　　To a loud 'Praise God!' broke
And roll'd up to the azure cloud
　　And roll'd off to the main,
And oaths, by Him, that day, they vowed
　　Set off a dreadful train.

" The Quaker atmosphere was charged
　　With spirit, as never, where
The heavenly-hearted Penn had warred
　　With only beads and prayer,
But meekness could n't endure the ring
　　Of the king's balls,—to stake her
Pluck against these, was sure to bring
　　The volunteering Quaker.

" The tune of the old bell was heard
　　Up in the pines of Maine ;
It sped the coast, too, like a bird,
　　Down to the Mexic main ;
'T was caught in Carolina's swamps ;
　　It woke up Eutaw Springs ;
To it the British regular tramps
　　When it at Cowpens rings.

" The old bell hurries to declare
　　How, with the drum's tattoo—

When rolling up the Delaware
    Came on the hurrying foe,—
It called the sires and sons to arms,
    It beat the reveillé,
But lost its breath pounding alarms
    When Howe sailed in from sea.

"The Sabbath bells all play'd the air,
    Such wond'rous love was in it;
The Union learned its common prayer,
    When parson Jefferson blessed it:
And where the dove-of-peace can come
    To nestle with the eagle,
There, Love and Freedom find a home
    And men can worship equal.

" We carried the key-note, which was found
    To cheer the gallant crew,
With this, the gallant ship did bound
    Across Old Ocean blue,
Before Key had her rhythm wrote
    The sailor loved to scan her
Wild whistling music, note by note,
    Of the Star Spangled Banner.

" Before this master found the scale
    And wrote her starry tune
Our Banner proved the favoring sail
    Which flew before the sun;
With this, our tars the guns could slip
    On every enemy's cruiser,

Lawrence did never give up the ship,
 Perry's sea-fight was a bruiser.

" It was the Spirit of the Bell
  That started up the fray,
Tripping the foemen when they fell
  At Resaca d'la Palmá ;
Through blasts of death it led away,
  It led out of the ditch,
And with the foe at Monterey
  It was a very witch.

" When the golden crown has fallen
  From the proud Chapultepec,
Leaving Mexico an orphan
  And her gloamy age a wreck,
Up among her white Sierras
  Floats this air from drum and fife,
Like a storm swoop down the cheerers,
  Swoop our heroes to the strife.

THE NEW BELL.

" HARK, hark, to the new Liberty Bell
  From the dome of Liberty Hall !
The tale we volunteer to tell
  Rings round this starry ball !
The boys all know the Hancock march
  The girls the Lincoln prayer,
But every Union pitch we search
  For Farragut's lyre there.

" When he was up among the ropes
　　Lash'd to the main-top spar,
Where for the Rebel ram he gropes
　　He flashed out like a star!
And clearly, over the booming guns
　　And yell of shot and shell
A strain of hero-music runs
　　Which struck sparks from the bell.—

" When bright and glancing rays of steel
　　Went flashing up Lookout,
The boys in blue did never reel
　　Before their foemen stout,
And every hero did his work
　　As right before his eyes
Hooker and Grant and every Turk
　　Were bound for Paradise.

" And when a stream of fire and shell
　　Pour'd out of Wagner, grim,
The memory of our solemn knell
　　Mov'd ev'ry heart with him,
When, DuPont bared his brow, and stood
　　With God's hands on his head—
Vowing to make the Union good,
　　Or give his life instead.

" And when flint Thomas stood against
　　The Rock of Chickamauga,
There was a roll of bass commenced
　　The hero alone could augur,

And when the gunner's tuning-forks
   Struck their antiphony,
It woke an echo 'mong the rocks
   Which rung a victory.

" And on the bell, and on the bell
   The strokes were fleetly falling,
Fast as the concuss'd shot they fell
   The fun was never palling,
And never since the Union gun
   Scattered the enemy,
Did the Bell's clapper ever run
   The tune so merrily.

" The bell for victory insane
   When dinging like a jester,
Its tympanum caught the refrain
   The gallop from Winchester,
' Face about, boys, we're going back,
   We're going back to lick 'em ! '
Struck it with such a sudden thwack
   It shrieked out ' Double quick 'em !'

" Our plumy banners road along
   The winds, like a free eagle ;
When, up the sun rose bright and strong
   The Union stars looked regal,
And when the day and darkness met
   Over those Southern regions,
Our stars did never, never set
   With Sherman and his legions."
*   *   *   *   *

These songs, like a long *quipu* cord,
   Knot up a hundred years;
Back—when the painted savage warr'd
   Like his brother beast, appears
The conquering crew that pressed their way
   Through walls of waters wide,
Overthrowing Nature's strong array
   In arms, on every side.

Then, through the leafy windows pour
   Of temples vast and high,
The notes that came to Freedom's shore
   In the bell of Liberty;
And hymns to God went singing through
   Old aisles unused to such,
They turn'd the stately forest to
   The school-house and the church.

The winds were busy with the sails
   That sought this distant shore,
The new discover'd soil unveils
   Its thousand springs, which pour
Into the waiting hands that spread
   The gifts with magic thrift,
And Industry and Genius wed
   And Art and Skill they lift!

Wherever now, we wend our way,
   If toward the Northern gates
And try their icy locks, or stray
   To the sun-pasture States,

Or look for the prairie flowers,
　Or seek f r golden sand,
The Independence Bell there showers
　Its music on the land.

THE OLD AND THE NEW—JULY 4, 1876.

A HUNDRED years with all their freight
Are rolling out of sight,
The centuries take another mate
On their eternal flight,
It came and found the gates ajar
Which open on the east,
It blazoned each name with a star,
Thirteen!—gloriously increased;—
It came and cast its flashing crown
Down from its radiant brow,
And called on God to send renown
As its deserts allow,
It hurled its scepter from its hand,
It seized a pen of flame
And wrote its oath so strong, the land
Saw its prophetic name,
It plead for "Progress, Truth, and Right"
With all which these entail,
And held its glittering sword in sight
To break—when these prevail;
It came with rudely armed men
From hillside and from plain,
The farm, the mill, the work-shop, then
The school in which they train,

They had no manual of arms
But practiced with a foe
Who filled the forest with alarms,
As winter with the snow.

Our dear! Our dear! forefathers, who
Died through these hundred years,
Our filial gratitude will show
Its blossoms as appears—
Wherewith to deck your scattered graves
Where, rescued by your name,
The grass that waves above their caves,
Is whispering your fame.

We love you for the toiling hand
And busy, patient brain
Which broke the soil and turned the land
To traffic's golden gain;
We love you for the worrying thought
Which tired nature down,
For every crude invention wrought
In rudest wood and stone;
We love you for the wrestling boor
Who felled the forest trees
And piled the walls and laid the floor
Of puncheon out of these,
Who toiled with rifle at his side
Watching for lurking death,
And yet his courage never died
But with his final breath,

Who saw his household growing strong
Although by danger shorn,
Whose maids were cheered with rustic song
And kissed when husking corn ;
We love you for the acts of faith
Which made our fathers one,
For what your backwoods' prayer convey'th
Which led the preacher on,
The scattered settlers' flag of smoke,
The blazing ax they swung
Were heralds of the light that broke
Where the Good Tidings rung.

How could they ever think to lay
The broad foundations down
Of such a government, as they
Left us, to rear upon ?
So few, so weak, so much in need
Of money, power, and fame,
Surely, they were the chosen seed
To whom the blessing came.

They guarded the pomerium[1]
The little Mayflower plowed,
Within the stronger walls have come
Now, the amassing crowd,
They were the dress of many lands,
They talk like many men
And all put forth their brawny hands
To heave our anchor then,

And when they cast it in the sea
Of politics, our ship
Rides out the angry waves as free
As the storm-petrel's dip.

A hundred years put forth their strength
And lo! the mighty change,
Steam strides now twenty leagues, its length
An hour, across our range,
The little boat which floated on
Our rivers, like a shell,
Now nestles 'midst the reeds, or gone
Down 'neath the turgid swell
The iron-lunged leviathan
Raises with blasts of breath,
Vanquishing many a haughty clan
Whose heart-breaks found them death.

A hundred years put forth their wealth
And lo! the mighty show ;—
A thousand industries,—our health,
We see rise up, and go,
Our unknown values—till the Type
And spiritual Press
Gave to the Century in our grip,
Their Autographic dress.

With giant progress at the helm
Our hundred years have run
And opened wide the western realm
And passed out with the sun ;

The Asiatic lands have heard
And seen our pond'rous train,
These dead, within their graves have heard
And wakened up again,—
We hail the true prophetic day
Of the millennium song,—
Their despots tremble at our sway
And cower before their wrong.

[1] Pomerium—A space around the walls of a city or town. It was anciently laid off with a plow.

MY COUNTRY—A THRENODE:

WRITTEN during the corruption of public officials by the Whisky
Ring, the winter of 1875-76.

My Country! name for that sweet lyre
    Which gives the soul its noblest thrill,
What other theme can so inspire?
    What song is so enrapturing still?

My earliest Muse, thy suasive voice
    Which moved the land from end to end,
When Virtues stirred thee to rejoice,—
    When Evils rous'd thee to forefend.

When list'ning to thy chords divine,
    And few, thy story, then could mar,—
We owned their sweet concord—" the sign
    Of Order "—was thy first great law.

While all the adjunctives that wait
    Like ministers about this throne,
Bespeak thy dignity of state,
    Adding their luster to thine own.

Behold how easy Learning's point
    Cuts the shale of Ignorance to-day;
Wisdom comes newly from the mint
    Contending sternly for her sway;

Behold how Genius snaps our chains,
  Unfetters all the laboring hands,
And only asks for her sweet pains
  The friendship which her love commands;

Behold how lightly Labor lifts   .
  The rock, and earth, and yellow ore,
How lightly o'er our broad fields, sifts
  The seed and brings it to our door;

Behold how lightly fly the wheels,
  Behold how lightly ply the ships,
Behold how lightly it unreels
  The railway, where the carriage trips.

My Country in thy earlier hours
  Vocal with patriotic songs,
How all their grandest music pours
  Thy flashing defiance, of wrongs !—

How every rood of land, that owned
  The name Columbia, we loved,
How our Republic was renowned
  For unity, in which we moved !—

What if there was a cloud or two
  Between us and the effulgent sun !
The fairest sky we ever view
  Will have some shadows o'er it run.

My Country, I would sing to thee
  A true, an earnest, wailing strain,

Flattery would mar its harmony,
  Then honest! though it brings me pain.

But thou art sad!   Thou canst not see
  Unsought, the clean, the just, the strong,
With trembling consciences men flee
  Where Guilt stalks with its glass along.

"*Et tu Bruté!*" thy breaking heart
  Hast uttered, with each falling stroke,
Thou art no tyrant, but the part
  Of tyrants, bows thee to their yoke.

My Country thou art sad!   And I
  Have sought the meaning of thy grief,
Thou canst not put thy Reason by,—
  Thou must have for thy wrongs relief.

Thou hast a hideous viper laid
  Too near thy vitals, thou *must* see!
Each branch of thy official aid
  Is poisoned with rank perjury.

Thou hast the reprobate and vile
  And cruel in thy posts of trusts,
Thy asylums reeking with guile
  And victims shackled in the dust.

My Country, I had sung to thee
  A sweeter song in other times,
I wait the turn of destiny
  To sooth thee with a lover's rhymes.

For lovers can not always praise !
  The Truth should be thy altar's flame,
Another torch's flickering blaze
  Would leave thy heaven obscured the same.

And I would sweep thy heaven serene
  Counting the stars upon thy sky ;
Were this fair Western World a queen
  Would crown her with my own Country.

SOUVENIRS.

AT MY FATHER'S GRAVE.

With filial reverence, I muse above
This hillock, mingling with the dust I love,
From the grave's trance, its noble form revived,
The kind, impartial kiss, the look of pride
As to his bosom I was fondly pressed
And all his dear, paternal love expressed;
All? No; such love is deeper than the sea,
Higher than the sky, and broader still, must be
Than that eternity of space, where go
The stars no telescope can ever show.
Paternal love! None ever said " How deep?"
But felt a stronger billow onward sweep,
Till love o'erwhelmed the body and the soul,
And only heaven can be the objective pole
Where we can feel we love, and where express
In satisfying words, our blessedness.

Stripped of the meretricious, false and vile,
How looks the soul without a spot or soil?
Judgments of men are naught before heaven's God,
The false, exposed by his purifying rod—
Not labor, poverty, nor lack thereof
Of those adornments, without which, men scoff;

One hand no whiter than another's there,
God asks "the virtue with which toil did share;"
And thy rough hand is whiter to me now
Than her's who wields a pen and seams the brow
With thought! Thine, a heroic daring in
The world's Olympiad, its bright crown to win;
And she, who loved thee, strives for one less fair,
Albeit mine is a wreath, and thine the rare
And heavy diadem of one who drew
The "sword from the plowshare," taking in lieu
Rewards of heaven—and not of men as I,—
But patiently waiting till thine hour to die.

God has so made us, each shall live for each,
None for himself. A broader love did teach
'That one forgiveness reaches all mankind;"
Bearing this hopeful charity in mind
We know the realm of heaven is full of love,
Sweeter than the lilies—fonder than the dove,
Each soul. And thine, dear father, thine how fair!
Each gift unfolded like a rose in air,
Shedding its radiance on the angels round,
Drinking the spirtual light that's always found
In heaven. Father, on thy love I grew,
And child-like grieve, years lost, the love I drew.
PEORIA, *May* 11, 1882.

FRIENDS' BURYING-GROUND.

THE Deed to the burying-ground adjoining the Friend's meeting-house, Woonsocket, R. I., bears date "17th December, the 6th of the reign of King George, the year of our Lord, 1719," described as "being the piece of land whereon is a burying-ground for the people called Quakers." This interesting fact was kindly furnished by Richard Battey, clerk of Smithfield monthly meeting, October, 19, 1883.

ASHES to ashes, dust to dust—
Here man ponders the lesson of trust,
"Till the angel of Life calleth over these tombs
And the dead shall ascend from funereal glooms.

How loyal to God is the dust that's here found;
Though, the King claimed his *fee* after deeding the
        ground,
The Quaker affirmed, with the force of an oath,
That a king is but man, and God sovereign of both!

The Sign Manual of royalty flourished apace,
And the Quaker permitted a burial place
As a favor to take and a privilege to ask,
Though the sins of a king e'en the grave can not mask.

For the cut of his coat and the brim of his hat,
His dialect plain as the scriptural fact,
For the spirit inspiring the prayer which he said,
He is lying apart for the Judge of the Dead!

God is all in this place, where no stone does record
The boast of a deed or the pride of a word,

For the Quaker is meek, and is lying apart
From the trappings of wealth and the splendor of art.

For the Judge of the Dead, what are plaudits and fame?
Though the world wave its palms and hosannas acclaim,
In the judgment of God how men's laurels will fade
And the prince be uncrowned, and the beggar be paid.

For the Judge of the Dead, what are marbles and
    bronze
That a touch thrills with life and a thought fills with
    tones?
The temples of Egypt, the pyramids, tombs,
Find their graves in the sand which the shifting wind
    combs.

For the Judge of the Dead, what are beauty and pride?
The stars are His work, and their glory beside;
All the beauty we boast, like their brightness must
    shine
With the light that is borrowed from Beauty Divine.

Here the proudest secure what the humblest may crave,
The presence of God and the rest of the grave;
God is all in this place, for these hillocks depend
On no favors of rank and no praises of friend.

With her mantle of holiness nature will screen
The dead who await Him, in slumber serene.
Rest in peace! Like the tents of old Israel spread,
These standards wave holily over each head.

Rest in peace !   While this spot is an Arimathea
God's angels are watching the sepulchres here,
Till these stones roll away and these bodies ascend
From the grave full of night to the day without end.

From this rest I go back to the world and its cares
And vanities, bait for its thousand of snares,—
I am Thine !   From the heart of a Quaker I came
And my song was inspired by her spiritual flame !

MY MOTHER.

My mother, when I knew that thou wast dead
The past swept by me, with her velvet tread,
A semblance of thy person, radiant, fair
And the rich beauty of thy girlhood, there ;
Author of my life and of my being, here,
Gone from us now—past years will reappear
Like shining comforters from heaven's walls,
When recollection thy dear name recalls.

Called by thy love, my infant years appear,
Maternal kisses sing around mine ear,
Following the guidance of thy loving hand,
Drinking the tones thy loving words command,
Returning thine, mine love, then innocent,
Thou, the good angel of my youth's content,
Alas, that childhood should survive its bliss,
To vex thee with my faults—which follow this.

As God's dear bosom shares each new-born one
The precious love, which from His breast does run,

Thy precious love shared each his sweet supply
And yet the fount of love was never dry,—
Mingled with my tears, did still unbittered flow,
Forgiveness healed each wound, and kissed each blow,
The saint to whom we prayed, with each complaint,
Though church and canon may not make the saint.

Thy fertile mind—with every year I grew
My mind expanding, every moment drew;
My precious guide, e'en in those real things
Which age and reason and experience brings;
Truer in council than all other friends;
Fervent and steadfast whate'er change portends;
Partner in sorrow, comforter in grief,
Thy touch, thy smile, thy look were my relief.

How rich and full the heart which sheltered me!
When my dear children clung around thy knee
Thy love has nursed them, as the noon-day sun
Nurses the violets which the shade has grown,
Trusting thy smiles as though they were mine own,
Catching affection in thy look and tone;
Easing my burdens, thou didst doubly bear
Thine own with thy sweet uncomplaining air.

How warm and free then flowed my sympathy
When these emotions drew me close to thee,
These pangs, these joys,—I learned to my surprise
I had not known thee, with my girlish eyes,
Until our hearts were knit by maternal knots
And common cares made our common lots

I never knew how strong thy love could be
Since first my life awoke thy love for me.

How thy frail strength was exercised for me;
And oh, how pure thy noble heart must be;
Chasing all shadows from before my life,
Making earth better, heaven with brightness rife,
Cheerful among present things—so apt to cloy,
Picturing the future as a time of joy,
Thy song celestial—where the saints do come
Must still continue the sweet strain of home.

When kneeling by thy bed of pain, I knew
The crucifying thought thy frail life drew,
Smoothing thy brow as though in sweet repose,
Folding thy hands as though a prayer arose,
Thou wouldst not see me weep—and did control
The pangs which pierced thee to the very soul;
Mother! when draining death's cup to the lees,
Thou couldst have died to spare thy children these.

O God, forgive us every thought amiss;
Forgive each word which stung a heart like this;
Forgive each deed which could have brought it shame;
Forgive each memory which we blush to name;
O make us faithful to the trust we have;
Deserving of the friends our heart must crave;
Honoring forgiveness! trustful, then in heaven
To clasp her who left no fault unforgiven.

    PEORIA, ILL., *May* 20, 1881.